A Thorny Path by Hesba Stretton

Hesba Stretton was the pen name of Sarah Smith who was born on July 27th 1832 in Wellington, Shropshire, the younger daughter of bookseller, Benjamin Smith and his wife, Anne Bakewell Smith, a devout Methodist. Although she and her elder sister attended the Old Hall school in town, they were largely self-educated.

Smith became one of the most popular Evangelical writers of the 19th century. She used her "Christian principles as a protest against specific social evils in her children's books." Her moral tales and semi-religious stories, mainly directed towards the young, were printed in huge numbers.

After her sister submitted, without her knowledge, a story on her behalf ('The Lucky Leg', was a bizarre tale of a widower who proposes to women with wooden legs) Smith became a regular contributor to Household Words and All the Year Round, two popular periodicals begun by Charles Dickens. Dickens would collaborate with many writers to produce his part-work stories. Smith writing under the pseudonym Hesba Stretton (created from the initials of herself and four surviving siblings: Hannah, Elizabeth, Sarah, Benjamin, Anna and the name of a Shropshire village; All Stretton) contributed a well-regarded short story, 'The Ghost in the Cloak-Room', as part of 'The Haunted House'. She would go on to write over 40 novels.

Her break out book was 'Jessica's First Prayer', published in the Sunday at Home journal in 1866 and the following year as a book. By the end of the century it had sold over one and a half million copies. To put that into context; ten times the sales of 'Alice in Wonderland'. The book gave rise to a strand of books about homeless children in Victorian society combining elements of the sensational novel and the religious tract bringing the image of the poor, under-privileged, child into the Victorian social conscious.

A sequel, 'Jessica's Mother', was published in Sunday at Home in 1866 and eventually as a book, some decades later, in 1904. It was translated into fifteen European and Asiatic languages as well as Braille, depicted on coloured slides for magic lantern segments of Bands of Hope programmes, and placed in all Russian schools by order of Tsar Alexander II.

Smith became the chief writer for the Religious Tract Society. Her experience of working with slum children in Manchester in the 1860s gave her books great atmosphere and, of course, a sense of authenticity.

In 1884, Smith was one of the co-founders, together with Lord Shaftesbury and others, of the London Society for the Prevention of Cruelty to Children, which then combined, five years later, with societies in other cities to form the National Society for the Prevention of Cruelty to Children. Smith resigned a decade later in protest at financial mismanagement.

In retirement in Richmond, Surrey, the Smith sisters ran a branch of the Popular Book Club for working-class readers.

Sarah Smith died on October 8th, 1911 at home at Ivycroft on Ham Common. She had survived her sister by eight months.

Index of Contents

Chapter I

In Kensington Gardens

It was a dark, dreary November day, with not a break in the clouds. The naked branches of the trees in Kensington Gardens crossed each other in a network of black lines against the grey and gloomy sky. There had been a dense fog in the morning, but it had lifted a little, and you could see the thick clouds overhead; and the closely-planted trunks of the trees crowding together. Underfoot lay a brown carpet of fallen leaves, rotting under the constant dripping of moisture from the boughs above them. The air was not cold, but it was damp, and there seemed no life in it. The short afternoon had begun, yet there were no groups of children playing in the long vistas and broad paths of the Gardens. The thick drizzle of a November day had kept most people prisoners at home.

There were a few passers-by, however, who made their way hurriedly along the soft wet walks, with no sauntering footsteps, or wandering glances on the dismal scene around them. They were all too much occupied with their own discomfort to pay much heed to a melancholy little group, which, with sad and slow steps, loitered along under the dank moist trees. A woman, whose lugged clothing clung about her, was the centre of it. She carried on one arm a baby some few months old, whilst with the other hand she led an almost barefooted child of three years. A blind old man walked at her side, guiding himself by keeping his withered hand upon her shoulder. Neither the old man nor the little girl got on quickly; and very slowly the faltering, wearied footsteps of this little knot of poverty and suffering passed along one of the by-paths. Even the child's prattle was stilled for the time by weariness and-hunger; and no sound except the baby's half-formed words broke the silence among them.

"Where are you leading us to, Hagar?" asked the old man, after a while.

She made no answer. The moment was come at last when despair had gained full possession of her. She had been struggling hard for a living ever since her husband had died, six months ago, just as the summer was coming, with its lighter hardships and fewer claims. But now winter had set in, and the burden of this old man leaning on her shoulder, and the child dragging at her hand, was too heavy for her. She had turned aside into the almost deserted Gardens, because she could no longer endure to see the stream of people along the main road, all of them hastening to get their work done, and hurry home to their own fireside. There was neither work nor home for them. Her own hands might have kept herself and her baby, but she had been unable to earn enough for her father and her little girl. All was gone now, even the poor shelter of the bare room, for which she could no longer pay the rent. There was nothing left but to starve together.

"Father!" she said, after a long pause, and speaking in a loud hoarse whisper, as if ashamed and afraid of being overheard, "you couldn't make up your mind to go to the poor-house for a bit?"

"I'd lie down and die like a dog first," he answered passionately.

He had said the same words often; but Hagar's heart was hardened by them, as it had never been hardened before. Many and many a time had she given him more than his share of their hardly-earned food, and when he still asked for more, she had taken the morsel off her own plate, and gone hungry and famished herself. She had parted with all her own spare clothing, before she had touched one article of his. She had toiled and slaved for him. Yet, now they were homeless and penniless, he gave the same old answer; his pride would not bend, if she and her children died for it.

"Die like a dog!" There was nothing but that before them, if they did not go into the workhouse. "It is better to die than to live," she muttered to herself. The baby's fingers played about her face, but awoke no smile upon it. The blackness of despair was all about her. She looked up, and saw only the unbroken and deepening gloom of the clouds, behind which the winter sun was going down rapidly, with night following swiftly in its track. Her little girl dragged more heavily at her hand, and the blind old man, groaning and stumbling at her side, seemed to lean more of his weight upon her shoulder. She could bear it no longer. Surely the baby was load enough for her.

"Dot," she said, stopping suddenly, "run round those trees there, and see what you can find. Father, stay here a minute tilt I come back."

She did not wait for any word of peevish remonstrance from the wearied old man, but dropped the child's hand, and shook off his chose grasp. Swiftly and noiselessly on the thick carpet of dying leaves, she hurried away. She did not dare to turn round for a last glance. More and more quickly grew the distance between them, until at last she began to run as one afraid of some pursuer, and ran breathlessly to lose herself among the busy. throng of people in the main road. She had thrown off her burden.

The blind man stood still in the path where she had left him, tapping the ground with his stick to feel for the roots of the trees, over which he feared to stumble. Two or three persons passed him, but no one spoke. Very soon he grew impatient, and listened eagerly for Hagar's return, with his grey head bent down, and his hand to his ear to catch the faintest sound of her approaching footsteps. But he could hear nothing, save the ceaseless roll of wheels passing along the streets, and the low splash of the rain drops falling from the branches overhead; the few feet passing to and fro made no sound until they were close upon him, and then he knew they were not hers. At length he lifted up his head and called:

"Hagar! Hagar! Hagar!"

It was strange and thoughtless of her to go so far out of hearing, and leave him there in the way of passers-by. It was high time, too, that she found some place for them to put their heads into for the night. It must be getting late; he felt how dreary the gloom of the evening was, though he could not see the darkness of the sky.

"Hagar!" he called again, in a louder voice, "Hagar!"

There was no voice calling back again, strain his ear as he might to catch it. His uneasiness deepened into a vague dread. At all times his blindness made him lonely; but now his loneliness seemed an utter and fearful solitude, as if he had been abandoned in some wilderness, unknown to any human being. Where was he? How was he to move on, and reach any place of refuge, thus left to himself? He groped about with his stick, and touched only the trees, which seemed to hem him in. All around him he could hear the stir and roar of busy life; but he could not find his way to it. He had never realised before what Hagar had been to him.

"Hagar!" he cried for the third time.

No answer. He would have been angry had not tears come into his sightless eyes, and sobs into his throat. He leaned his head against the rough bark of the tree under/which he was standing, and wept bitterly. He began to ask himself, was it possible that he was really forsaken? Or was Hagar only gone away in a sulk, keeping aloof for a little while, to make him feel how helpless and dependent he was Perhaps, if he could only see, he would find her sitting down on one of the benches a little way off, waiting till she thought he was punished enough. Ah! if he could only see!

"Where's my mother?" asked a little voice, close beside him.

"Is that you, Dot?" he asked, eagerly.

"Yes, it's Dot that's here," answered the little girl "where's my mother?"

"Can't you see her anywhere?" he said, clasping the child's cold hand in a firm grasp, lest he should lose her again. "Look all about you, Dot, among the trees, and tell me can't you see her?"

"No, no," sobbed the little child, "Dot can't see her nowhere; and I want her. Dot's so hungry."

"Hagar Hagar!" he shouted, at the highest pitch of his weak old voice; and Dot called "Mother!" in her shrill young tones. Then they listened for a minute in silence, standing together hand in hand under the wintry trees.

"She's gone!" groaned the old man, dropping the hand of his little grandchild, and letting his stick fall to the ground. The despair that had conquered Hagar was catching him in its toils. What was to become of him now? He was old and blind; homeless and penniless. He had often sworn to lie down, and die like a dog, rather than go into the workhouse. But it is no easy thing to die. Death will not come when he is called. The most wretched man cannot die when he will, or as quickly as he will. Now Hagar had deserted him, there was nothing before him but the dreaded and hated workhouse.

Chapter II

Help in Need

Half all hour passed by, and night was fast closing in; yet, still the blind old man and the little child were waiting, in their utter helplessness, under the dark trees. Now and then a faint ray of hope gleamed on tile old man's despair, as he heard a step drawing near, and fancied it might be Hagar's, coming back to them. He would not move from the spot where she had left him, for fear of her missing them in the dusk. Dot cried softly to herself; having been taught not to cry aloud lest grandfather should hear her and be angry. She was the more miserable because he held her hand so fast that she could not stir from his side. He was constantly asking her if she could not see her mother; and the shivering, hungry child saw nothing but the tall black trunks of the trees, standing thickly around them, and growing blacker every minute.

At last a brisk step was heard, and a boy's loud whistling coming close to them. The footstep stopped on the path beside them, and a boy's sharp voice spoke to them.

"Hallo! Mister," he said, "the gates are bein' locked, and you'll be turned out soon. If you're tired, I'll carry your little gel for you as far as we go together. What's she cryin' for, oh? Why, you're blind! Where's your dawg?"

The lad paused, and looked about him in sheer amazement. There was no dog to be seen, nor any one to lead the blind man. The little girl was too small and young to know her own way; and how could she get here, with a blind old man, in the heart of Kensington Gardens? He stooped clown and brought his sharp pale face on a level with the child's, who left off crying, and broke into a smile as she looked at him.

"She's gone!" moaned the old man, "she's left me to die like a dog."

"Who's she?" asked the boy.

"My daughter; Dot's mother," he replied. "She brought us here an hour ago or more; and she's gone away and deserted us. She wanted to put me in the poor-house—"

"Oh! don't you go there!" said the lad, eagerly, "don't you! It's worse than a prison; lots. Mrs. Clack says so. It 'ud be a sad pity for the little gel to go into the poor-house. You tell me where you live, and I'll lead you home; and may be she'll be sorry she forsook you by this. Folks do things without thinkin'. She'd never leave a little gel like this. There! you catch hold of my arm, and I'll lead you home to her."

"We've no place to go to," he said, "that's why Hagar has left us. They turned us out of our lodgings this morning."

"That's bad!" exclaimed the boy, falling back a step or two to contemplate the old man and the child, with his head on one side, and with an air of profound interest on his face. He could not find it in his heart to go away and leave them in the gloom and chill of the evening, never to know what had become of them. Plunging his hand into his pocket, he drew out a crust of bread, round which he had wound a bit of string; amid carefully unwinding it, he put the crust into Dot's hand, and watched her with curiosity, as she fastened her little teeth upon it.

"Hungry! why, that's bad again," he said; "if she was only a little dawg, I'd take her straight home with me to Mrs. Clack. Well! I couldn't leave 'em to be found dead in the morning, or to go to the poor-house, that's certain. Mister, will you and your little gel come along with me, and ask Mrs. Clack what we'd best do?" "Who's Mrs. Clack?" he asked.

"Don't you know Mrs. Clack?" cried the boy, "that lives down in Chelsea? Well, I do errands for her, and I'll take you along with me and see what she says. It's a good step, but I'll carry the little gel, and you can catch hold of my arm; and we'll go slow. Mrs. Clack likes little gels."

He lifted Dot tenderly in his arms, and bidding tile old man grip him hard and step out without being afraid, for he would guide him carefully, he led them along the path towards the gate, chatting gaily as they went.

What is your name?" asked the old man.

I never had what one 'ud call a proper name," he answered; "at least, not like other boys, you know; or, if I had, I lost it afore I can remember. But I call myself Don; and I won't answer to any other name. I'll tell you why. Folks kept callin' me anythin' they liked, till I didn't even know who I was. And there was a little dawg, a little black-and-tan terrier, as sharp as a needle, that used to run up to me and sniff round me and eat a bit out o' my hand, as if we'd known each other all our lives; and the lady as belonged to him called him Don. I heard her once call him away from me: 'Don, Don!' she said; and that was the very last time I ever saw hum. I never set eyes on that little black-and-tan dawg again. So I chose his name for my own, and it often makes me think of him comin' up so friendly and familiar. That's how I came to call myself Don. I s'pose, mister," suggested Don, half timidly, "you'd not mind tellin' me your name?"

"My name is John Lister," he replied. "I'm come down in the world, young sir, lower than I could ever have dreamed of. I've been first violin in popular theatres, and drawn as much as a pound a night. We did well, young sir, very well, till my violin was broken in a street row; and Hagar's husband died after a long illness which drained our exchequer. Could a man such as I am stoop so low as to enter a poor-house?"

"No, no!" cried Don, eagerly and respectfully, "you must never think of such a thing. I'm fond of music, I am. P'raps Mrs. Clack has got a fiddle in her stores somewhere. She don't know half what she's got. If there's a fiddle you'd be set up again, wouldn't you? I wish I'd come sooner, and saved Mrs. Hagar from goin' away and leavin' you. You'll be all right, now you are goin' to Mrs. Clack. She's the cleverest woman in London, and she'll know what to do. We shall be there sooner than you think."

The old man's mind was fast falling into a state of confusion and bewilderment; and as he dreamily walked along, he scarcely heard the flow of Don's words, mingled with the din of the streets through which they were passing. He began to fear that he had made a fatal mistake; and that Hagar had left him and Dot only for a little while, perhaps to buy bread, or to seek a shelter for the night, and that she would return to the spot where she had left them to find them gone. Was it probable that his own daughter would desert him? For nearly thirty years she had been at his beck and call, serving him with unfailing patience. Could she fail him now, in this bitter extremity? He had grown so accustomed to having her about him, that he could not realise that she had at last forsaken him. He stopped short on the pavement, and set his grey, blind face once more in the direction of Kensington Gardens.

"I must go back," he said sharply, striking the pavement with his stick, "my daughter will be searching for us."

"No, no," answered Don. "Why, the gates were closed after us, as we came through; and nobody 'ud be let in after that. You told me she'd left you to die like a dog, didn't you? I couldn't have done it myself, never! But nobody can tell why she did it; and never you fret. You come along to Mrs. Clack, and if she's got a fiddle in her stores, I'll guide you to lots o' quiet streets, where the p'lice lets you alone. You'll play on your fiddle, and you'll pick up a sight more than your livin'. I've known blind fiddlers take shillings sometimes; and Dot's such a pretty little gel, she'll make folks' hearts soft, I know. Come, now! Don't you fret. Never care for nothin' I say."

Old Lister went on feebly; sobbing now and then as a child does, when his fit of crying has been over some time ago. He was chilled to the bone, and faint with hunger. It was well, perhaps, that he could not see the turn Don took at last, under an archway which led into a blind alley at the back of a low and squalid street. It was an old mews, but it was no longer used as coach-houses and stables, with the rooms over them forming the dwelling-places of grooms and coachmen. The low buildings were partly falling into ruins, or occupied by persons who could afford to pay only the lowest rents. The water dropping from the roofs on each side of this alley, ran into a channel in the middle, choked with dirt and refuse, along which Don picked his way, and guided the blind man's faltering steps as well as he could.

"Here's Mrs. Clack's," he said, cheerfully, as they reached the last building, an old two-stalled stable and a coach-house adjoining. The narrow staircase to the rooms above, built to admit one person only, was hung with an odd collection of clothing of all sizes and kinds. A glimmer of gas-light, no stronger than that of a rush candle, cast a dim and doubtful gloom upon them and Dot clung with both arms round Don's neck, as he carried her carefully upstairs.

"Mrs. Clack," he said, tapping softly at a door that stood ajar, and speaking in a, persuasive voice, "I've brought you a little gel, a good pretty little gel, as you'll he very fond of, I know; and her name's Dot! Dot and Don, you know. You've got lots of clothes that 'ill fit her, and I'll work harder than ever. And, Mrs. Clack," he went on, still more persuasively, "I've brought you her grandfather, a blind fiddler, that 'ill get, oh, lots o' money by fiddling in the quiet streets, if you happen to have got such a thing as a fiddle in the stores."

By this time Mrs. Clack had lit the gas in her room, and came to the door. She was a small, spare old woman, with a wrinkled face, still keeping a rosy tinge, as if she had lived most of her younger years in the fresh air and sunshine of the country. In the room behind her there was no portion of the walls to be seen for the numerous articles of clothing which hung upon them; whilst the four posts of Mrs. Clack's bed were clothed from head to foot in a full walking dress, as if they were so many persons about to set out at once into the streets. In the dim light the room looked full of tenants, though Mrs. Clack was living in it alone.

"Brought rue a little girl, Don!" she exclaimed, "and a man, Don! I wouldn't have minded a little girl; but whatever are we to do with a man? Oh, Don! you know I can't abide to have aught to do with men. They cost so much, and they're so wasteful and masterful. I have kept clear of 'em all these years; and now you've brought one of' 'em to my very door-sill. I'd rather you'd brought me ten dogs, than one man. Dear, dear, I can't abide a man!"

"Mrs. Clack," said Don, mournfully, "you know I'm bound to grow up into a man. I couldn't be turned into a woman, nohow. And he's a very old man, and blind; and he's hungry and cold, and his own daughter's run away and forsook him, and I couldn't leave him and Dot to be froze to death in the Gardens, could I? Bless you, it won't cost you nothin' just to give him a lodgin' for a little while, till he can turn hisself round. Only look how old he is! Scarcely like a man, you know. He won't be drinkin' and smokin', and wastin money. I told him you were the cleverest woman in London, and he must come and talk with you. Won't you just let him come in, and let's talk it over?"

The voices of Don and Mrs. Clack sounded in old Lister's ears like some indistinct buzzing. He stood tottering behind Dot and Don, shivering with hunger and all, and bewilderment, and as Mrs. Clack looked at him, he stretched out his shaking hands to her.

Don't let me die like a dog!" he cried.

"No, no, no!" answered Mrs. Clack, "poor old creature! Come along here. I couldn't turn him away, Don, though he is a man, poor fellow! Come in, and we'll do the best we can for to-night."

Chapter III

A Long Night

When Hagar gained the main road, and was lost in the stream of busy traffic, she went on her way mechanically, with swift steps, seeing none of the many faces she met, and hearing nothing of all the stir and noise about her. She had sunk into so profound a depth of wretchedness that she was conscious of nothing but her own misery. She had tasted no food since the night before, but she did not know she was hungry and faint. The slush of the muddy pavement was oozing through her worn-out boots, and the drizzle of the November evening penetrated through the thin dirty shawl she had crossed tightly over the baby, who was sleeping on her bosom. But Hagar did not say to herself that she was wet through, and cold. There was no shelter for her from the coming night, but she did not think of that. A blank despair, heavy and thick as the leaden clouds that hid the sky, hemmed her in on every side; and she felt only a vague unbroken sense of desolation. A faint, half-sleeping sob from the baby she was carrying was the first sound that brought her back to her present misery. She pressed it a little closer to her bosom, and her other hand fell down by her side, as if to catch hold of Dot's, whilst, almost against her will, she turned her head to see if she was anywhere near. She knew her child could not be pattering beside her, for she had not forgotten what she had just done. The image of her old father, blind and helpless, standing still under the trees, and of Dot running away to play at her own bidding, remained in her brain, and she could not get rid of it. By this time she had wandered a good way from Kensington Gardens, and had lost herself in a knot of streets; but quite clearly she seemed to see the tall bare trees, scattering heavy drops of rain from their wet branches, and the old man and little child forsaken amid wretched among them.

Hagar ventured to sit down to rest now and then in the quiet streets, and on the steps of some empty house, where she could remain undisturbed. Once she fell asleep. How long she slept she couldn't tell; but the baby's cries awoke her—those shrill cries of suffering which pierce a mother's heart. It was almost impossible to soothe the little creature and by the time it was slumbering again she was herself wide awake, and more keenly sensitive to her black despair. Yet she knew she must not sit there all night; so she bestirred herself, stretched her aching and stiffened limbs, and set out again on her aimless wandering with creeping footsteps; moving simply to keep life in her veins, for she had no home to go to, and knew of no shelter to seek.

If her father and Dot had been with her, she would have gone to the workhouse for their sakes; but for her own she did not care to go, nor for the baby's, who would perish with her, if she perished. It would not be a bad thing to die, she thought, if she could die peacefully in a bed, with quiet, gentle people about her, as her husband had died six months ago. But to freeze to death on some doorstep, or be carried away at the last moment to some hospital, amid strangers; that was hard! It would be dying like a dog, as her father so often said.

At length she found herself again in the high road, and close by Hyde Park, where it joins Kensington Gardens. There were lamps everywhere in time Park; but the Gardens were unlighted and locked up. She crept slowly along time broad drive, looking over to the black masses of the trees beyond the sunk fence. It was possible that her father and Dot were still in there, crouching asleep under some of those trees, or stumbling to amid fro amidst those black shadows. They might not have been seen by the policemen, in the quiet, unfrequented path where she had left them. She made her way over the wet grass, and called softly across the sunk fence. There were but few carriages, and still fewer foot passengers, along the broad drive and no policeman was in sight. Hagar dragged herself along by the edge of the Gardens, searching the thick darkness with her eyes, and straining her ears for some answer to her low, frightened call. Ah! if she could but hear their voices calling back to her!

But her dread grew stronger every moment. Coming upon a place in the wall where the boys had pulled out some of the bricks, in order to climb up it. She placed her feet in the lowest hole, and laid the baby safely on the green turf above it. It was easy then to make her way into the empty and silent glades of the Gardens.

There was something very wild and mournful about this solitude in the heart of the din and tumult of London. Here were no familiar lamp-lights sending streams of brightness down into the deep shadows which surrounded her. Her weary feet caught against the roots of the trees. Not a footstep beside her own broke the stillness, which seemed more still, because of the distant roll of wheels and the busy sounds of city life, which came as it were from afar to her ears. She felt as if she was in some other world; darker, colder, sadder even than the one she had left. The trees shut out the sky, and were blacker than it could ever be. She could not hurry on her search, for her limbs felt stiff; and the baby lay like a dead weight on her bosom. But yet she crawled along, shivering and heavy-hearted, to the spot where she had left her father and her little girl.

There was nothing to be seen when she reached the narrow by-path. But through the trees the water in the Round Pond, where children float their little boats by day, gleamed with a pale and ghostly light. In the dead hush of the place she could hear the tiny waves lapping against the stonework which enclosed them. Was it impossible that the blind old man and time little child she had forsaken might have strayed this way, and fallen into the sullen water? She recollected hearing of an aged workman having lost his way in a fog, whose corpse had been found there. She paced round and round the great pond, feeling half-asleep and half-dead, yet compelled to pore now and then over some speck floating on the surface, too far off to be distinguished clearly. Was that Dot's white little face showing just above the water, where the pale light seemed to lie? Or could it be her father's grey head? Or was it merely the reflection of some break in the clouds, which she could not see where she was standing?

Then with a moan she turned away to seek those she had lost among the trees; and fancying she could catch some sign of them, as she searched behind one black thick trunk after another. It did not seem long since she had played at hide-and-seek with Dot round the same trees—only that was in the summer sunshine, and whilst her husband looked on at the game. Was this search only a terrible dream? Once or twice she came upon a heap of leaves gathered about the roots of a tree, which looked almost like the figure of a prostrate man stretched upon the damp ground. If she could find her father and Dot lying dead somewhere, all she felt was a dull desire to lie down beside them and die too.

But her search was in vain. Sometimes she sat down to rest on the seats, and seemed to sleep a little while, but as soon as she aroused herself again, she set out once more on her wanderings round the glimmering yet black pool, and in and out among the dark moaning trees. Now and then she called, though her voice, unknown to herself, never rose above a whisper. That strange wild whisper, "Father! little Dot!" could not reach any ears. No ear but God's could catch that cry; no eye but His could see her misery.

There was not a sign of day-break when the gates were opened at five o'clock in the morning. The sun would not rise for nearly three hours yet; but Hagar felt herself disturbed by time occasional tread of a workman going past on his day's labour. As in a dream still she made her way to one of the gates to the north of the Gardens. She was benumbed and bewildered. The baby had been moaning for the last few hours, and though the low mournful sound filled her ears, she felt unable to do anything to lull and hush it. She did not know where she was going, or what she was to do. Like one blind amid deaf she staggered on into the road, still as dark as at midnight; when suddenly she heard the rattle of wheels close upon her, mingled with the trampling of a horse's hoofs, and time angry shout of its driver. But it was too late; she was already under the horse's feet, and knew and felt nothing beyond that.

Chapter IV

A Day of Sadness

At five o'clock in the morning there were not many people about, yet a little knot of working men and women quickly gathered about the cab. The driver had been driving fast, counting upon the road being clear at such an hour; and he had found it impossible to pull up his horse in time. A man, dressed in the uniform of a railway-guard, sprang in an instant from the cab, and was the first to pull Hagar and her baby from under the frightened and plunging horse.

It's a woman!" he cried, "with a child in her arms." A policeman marched up briskly to the spot, and turned the bright side of his lamp upon Hagar's face. The guard had lifted her out of the road on to the kerbstone, and kneeling down was keeping her from sinking to the ground. The light fell full upon her worn and haggard features and the thin drenched clothing clinging to her form. There was no sign of life about her, though her arms still clasped the baby tightly to her bosom. But the baby's pitiful wail had ceased for ever.

"Both dead!" said the, policeman.

"God forbid!" exclaimed the railway-guard, whose face wore an expression of anxiety. "Look here; take her sharp to the hospital, and lose no time about it. My name's Abbott; everybody knows me at Paddington. I'm just in with the night train, and my poor mother's on her death-bed. She was dying last night, when I started from Birkenhead; and I was hurrying home to see her once again, if she's alive yet. But here, lift the poor creature into the cab; I'll go home afoot. I'll come and see after her by-and-by.

He placed Hagar in charge of a woman who had been passing by on her way to work, and staying for a moment to watch the cab move off in the direction of the hospital, he started hurriedly onward to the home where his mother had been dying all the night, or was now lying dead. It had seemed a very hard and sorrowful thing to think of during the long hours of the journey, as the train he had charge of was rushing through the darkness, although to him it had seemed moving almost at a snail's pace. That had been his mode of life for several years, running down to Birkenhead one day, and coming back the next; spending only every other night, and every other Sunday at home. It was a life that suited him, for he was active and loved variety. He had found no fault with it until now, when his old mother, dearer to him than any other human being, was lying at death's door, and might have crossed the threshold with no last loving smile for him on her face, and no last good-bye from her dear lips.

Abbott turned into a quiet and pleasant street; dark this November morning, but, in summer days, when he came home at the same early hour, peaceful and shady, with trees planted before many of the houses, and flowers blooming on the window-sills. He and his mother had chosen to live here, in the area floor of a large house, rather than in a higher story of a dwelling in closer and busier streets. The upper portion of the house was occupied by a distant relative of theirs, who was a dressmaker. A few steps led down to their own separate door in the area, where some red leaves still fluttered on the Virginia creeper, which had made their front window green and shady in the late summer time. The front room was a large and pleasant kitchen; whilst the back room, where his mother slept, looked out on a little plot of grass, kept green and cool by her constant care of it. His own bed-chamber was up in the attics, to which he had to pass through his cousin's part of the house, where it was as quiet as it could be in London for his sleep through the morning hours. He had a latch-key to the area-door; though it had been seldom that he had not found his mother up, and his breakfast ready for him, as long as he had been able to get about at all. But this morning the place was dark as he turned his key carefully, and stepped noiselessly into the passage, with the cautious step of one who is afraid of disturbing some light sleeper. As he closed the door, his cousin appeared on the threshold of his mother's room, looking out with eyes red with weeping.

"She's just going," she whispered, "you'd have been too late in another few minutes. She's been almost fretting for you to come."

Abbott knelt down and kissed his mother's white face.

"Mother," he said, "are you going to leave me alone?"

"Ay, alone, my lad!" she murmured, "yet not alone, because God is with thee! Thou know'st that?"

"Surely," he answered, "surely! Hasn't He been with you and with me all our lives? But it will be lonesome, mother. Never to see your dear face, and never hear your dear voice! We've been so happy together, mother."

"Ay, he's been a good son, Lord," said the dying woman, fondly, "never a rough word from him, and never a cross look. Lord, Thou'lt bless him, and abide with him, and bring him safe to me when his time comes. I leave him with Thee, Lord."

"I shall come, mother; I shall come," said Abbott. "That's a good hope," he sobbed.

"A good hope," she repeated, smiling. Her wrinkled but placid face was as tranquil as it had ever been when she was falling asleep for the night; and her dim, sunken eyes gazed into his face with all the old fondness and cheerfulness he had been used to see there. Her hand rested in his, and tried to clasp it tightly for a minute or two; but very soon the feeble pressure ceased, and the withered fingers grew cold. Then the eyelids drooped over the failing eyes, and her voice fell very softly on his ear.

"I'm going—but he will—come—to me," she faltered.

It was all over; and a few minutes afterwards Abbott mounted the long staircase to his little attic under the roof. The day was not breaking yet, and the fog was growing thicker over the city. He sat down on the side of his bed, and rested his head upon his hands, with a dreary sense of utter loneliness pressing down upon him. From the day that his father died, twenty-five years ago, when he was a boy of ten, he had never spent any long portion of his life aloof from his mother. He had lived with her and worked for her. She had been a calm-tempered, wise-hearted woman; and the simple, perfect love of mother and son had never been disturbed between them. And now she was gone, and he was alone—with no one to think of on his journeyings to and fro, and no home to come back to at the close of each. For a home with no human companionship would be no home to him.

"I shall go to her, but she will not return to mop" he kept repeating, slowly and mechanically, to himself. He thought of Christ raising to life again the young man at Nain, who "was the only son of his mother, and she was a widow," and he thanked God for having spared him to his own widowed mother, whose life had been a happy and a peaceful one. But he could not as yet realise that she was actually gone; that the place downstairs was empty. He crept quietly down again, and stood in the dark passage, listening to the voices and the movements of the women in his mother's room. There was nothing he could do, not even go in and sit down beside the bed, and look at the grave and tranquil face sleeping its last sleep. At last the thought of the poor woman, knocked down, perhaps killed, on his way home, flashed across his mind.

"I'll go and see if there's anything to be done," he said to himself.

It was three hours since Hagar and her baby had been admitted into the accident ward of the hospital. But the baby had been carried at once to the dead room, and Abbott was told it would be very doubtful if the woman would recover. There was no clue to her name or dwelling-place; and he could give no information about her. But when they asked him what must be done with the dead body of the child, and he looked down at the puny wasted frame and the small white face, the tears that had been smarting under his eyelids, filled his eyes as if he had been gazing on his mother's dear features.

"I've a funeral from my house," he said, "and the coffin shall be made a little larger for the little creature. Perhaps the mother would fret over it being buried by the parish, if she comes to herself and asks after it. Send the baby to my house."

So when Abbott's mother was laid in a coffin, her snow-white hair braided softly against her withered face, the little unknown child was placed beside her with its tiny head resting on her arm. The neighbours, who came in to see, said it was like Abbott and his mother, ever ready to give help and shelter to the friendless and homeless. The dead woman was sharing even her coffin and her grave with one who had no claim upon her, except that of being a child of the same heavenly Father.

Chapter V

Forsaken

There had been no break in Abbott's mode of life, excepting for the one day of the funeral; he went on travelling down to Birkenhead one day, and coming back the next, but everything seemed changed and saddened to him. There were many faces of travellers recognised from seeing them time after time; he exchanged friendly greetings, and gave kindly service to many whose names he did not know; but there was no longer a home for him. To go back to the rooms his mother had left empty was dreary and joyless. It grew yet more solitary when all his mother's little possessions were given away, in accordance with her own wishes, amongst several poor acquaintances. For what would be the use, she had asked him cheerfully, of keeping her gowns and shawls, and under-clothing till they were all rotten and moth-eaten, while there were so many poor folks needing them, with the winter coming on, when they would be more valuable? Yet it gave Abbott a pang to see his mother's shawl and bonnet worn on a Sunday before his own eyes by a woman who was no more like his mother, he said to himself; than a way-side weed is like a garden flower. He had never thought how sorely he should miss her.

Every other day, when he returned to Paddington, he did not fail to inquire at the hospital close by after the unknown, miserable woman, who was lying there in a long hand-to-hand conflict with death. There had been a concussion of the brain, and she had been unconscious for some days; even when she had somewhat recovered, the physician would not suffer her to be excited by being questioned, or told of her baby's death. There was no clue yet as to her name and history.

"Tell her Abbott's been asking after her," he said, as soon as they told him she was conscious; "not that she knows me, but it will be a pleasant thing to her to think that anybody cares how she's going on. There's nobody else but me to ask after her; and she isn't quite strange to me since her little child was buried in my mother's coffin."

It was several days before Hagar could understand the message, which was uttered very slowly and distinctly to her by the nurse, "Abbott has been asking for you." She lay quite still, answering nothing, and gazing with dim eyes into the nurse's face. "Abbott has been asking for you." They were the first words with meaning in them which reached her bewildered brain. By-and-by as she grew stronger, and her memory returned, she slowly pieced together the fragments of things remembered, so as to begin to understand that an accident had happened to her, and that she was in a hospital. But who Abbott was she did not know; yet there was a feeling of comfort conveyed to her every time she received his friendly message. She was a very silent patient, lying motionless and speechless for hours, with her dark eyes almost closed, and scarcely a look of life about her. Her mind was busily at work, however, groping about the darkened chambers of her brain, and recalling all her past career, from which she had been suddenly separated by a long interval of unconsciousness.

"I had a little baby," she muttered, half aloud, and the nurse, who was near to her, happened to overhear her.

"Yes, my poor dear," she said, kindly, "when you were knocked down, and injured so by a cab, you had a little baby in your arms."

"Where is she?" asked Hagar.

"It's where it will never know want any more," answered the nurse, laying her hand gently on Hagar's throbbing head, "never be cold any more, or hungry again. It's with Jesus, who said, 'Suffer little children to come unto Me, for of such is the kingdom of heaven.' Your baby is in heaven, my dear."

Hagar neither spoke nor wept; her thoughts were too busy for either words or tears. Baby was dead, and in heaven; but where was her old blind father, and little Dot? Something kept her back from asking the nurse, who, after lingering beside her a few seconds, went on to another patient, more clamorous for attention.

Hagar's mind had gone back to the moment when she had been knocked down, and felt the horse's hoofs upon her, and now it had travelled still farther back to the long and terrible night in Kensington Gardens. Then, suddenly, as if a vivid flash of lightning had shot across the darkness of a midnight sky, she seemed to see her father and Dot standing helplessly and forlornly under the leafless trees, as she had seen them last.

"I forsook them," she cried, starting up in bed, and speaking in a loud and bitter tone, "I forsook them, and now I'm forsaken. God has taken away my baby, and I'm left alone!"

When Abbott called the next day he was told that the unfortunate, unknown woman he inquired after was delirious, and little hope was felt for her life. Was the parish to bury her in the event of her death? He was the only person interested in her fate; and the question was referred to him.

"I've never seen her," he said," poor creature! and it's foolish of me, perhaps; but no! I can't leave her to be buried like a stray dog that nobody owns. I'd have liked to know something about her, though; but she'd have been alive yet, maybe, but for me taking a cab that morning. Leave it to me; I'll see she's buried decently."

But Hagar rallied again; though it seemed harder and more up-hill work to recover a second time. Very slowly and lingeringly she grew better; and most of the beds in the ward changed occupants more than once before she was well enough to receive a visit from Abbott, whose messages, faithfully delivered day by day, had comforted her with the feeling that she still had a friend in the outside world. It was on the first Sunda5r in the year, and the ward was crowded with friends of the patients, all quiet and conversing in whispers, when the nurse told Hagar that Abbott was come to see her. She lifted up her eyes, and looked inquiringly at the tall strong man, whose grave face met her gaze with an expression of friendly concern.

"I'm Abbott," he said, "the man whose cab knocked you down. I'm come to see what I can do for you; what amends I can make. My dear mother lay dying, and I was hurrying to get to her in time. It was a very foggy morning, and the driver did not see you."

"Did you get in time?" asked Hagar, faintly; "was your mother dead?"

"No, thank God!" he replied, "I was just in time; we said good-bye to one another. You know your little baby also died that same morning?"

Hagar's lips quivered as she nodded her head in silence.

"Yes," he said, softly, "that same morning the little blossom died; so I had it buried with her, in the same coffin. We could not ask your leave; but you wouldn't have said no to that?"

The tears were stealing down Hagar's cheeks; but there was almost a smile upon her white face.

"Oh! it was good of you," she murmured.

"Now," he said, after a little silence, and he spoke in a more cheerful and quicker tone, "let us know something about you. You've been lying here like a poor dumb creature that can't give any account of itself. Nobody knows your name, or where you come from; and your friends must think you are dead. There has been no one to ask after you save me. You will be well enough to be discharged in a week or two. Let me find your friends for you; or let me write to them."

"I haven't got a friend in the world," she answered; "I'm quite alone. Even God has forsaken me."

"No, no," he said, earnestly, "that is impossible; nobody is ever forsaken. You must not say that of God. But you had a home once?"

"Yes," she replied, "I had a home once, a happy home, and a husband, and two little children, and an old blind father, that I'd never left. But they are all lost, all lost arid gone."

"No one left?" be said, in a voice of deep compassion, that seemed to open her heart and lips, as she looked up into his pitying face with tearful eyes.

"Not one!" she cried. "I was going to drown myself if I dared. But there's always a judgment after death, and I was afraid of that. God is angry with those that go before He calls them Himself, and I was afraid, though I longed to die. I'm afraid of getting well now, and being turned out into the cold streets. What is to become of me? Where am I to go?"

She was getting excited, and her voice was growing high and shrill. The nurse came to the side of the bed, and shook her head warningly at Abbott.

"There then!" he said, soothingly, "don't be afraid, think of me as your friend. I'll prepare a place for you when you're well enough to leave the hospital. If my dear mother was living, it would be a joy to her to come and see you, and take you home with her. But there, be content. Nobody is ever really forsaken."

"God has forsaken me!" she answered.

"That is impossible," he said, again, "you are wrong in speaking so of God, your Father and my Father. Have you never heard what He says in His own book, 'Zion said, the Lord hath forsaken me, and my Lord hath forgotten me?' That is exactly what you are thinking in your own mind?"

"Yes," answered Hagar, eagerly.

"Ah!" he continued, smiling down upon her, "and now listen to what the Lord says to that, 'Can a woman forget her child? Yea, she may forget, yet will I not forget thee.'"

But as he spoke these words in a glad voice Hagar's face grew terrified and shocked. "Yes, I did forget," she cried in a loud key, which startled the quiet ward. Then she broke into a passion of sobs and tears, which shook her feeble frame sorely, and the nurse coming up quickly, bade Abbott, in a sharp and angry tone, to be gone at once.

Chapter VI

Mrs. Clack's Difficulty

Mrs. Clack felt herself very much put about and embarrassed by the presence of a man in her house. Old Lister had slept on Don's flock mattress in the coach-house below her dwelling-room, and Dot in her own bed beside her; but now Don had left the blind man in her charge while he was away at his daily work, and she did not know what to do with him. True, he was an old man and blind; but he was as strange, and almost as dreaded a creature to her, as if Don had brought one of the savage wild beasts from the Zoological Gardens to find a shelter in her quiet little home. She knew almost nothing of man and his ways. Though she called herself Mrs. Clack on her business cards, she had no actual claim to the title, for she was a single woman. She had been reared and trained in a small orphanage in the country, where sixteen orphan girls were brought up in strict, seclusion, never seeing any man nearer than the aged clergyman, who preached to them with the rest of his small congregation from the pulpit of the village church. She had never known her father, and she had had neither brother nor husband. Her first business had been that of a sempstress and dressmaker, mostly for servants, but as her sight began to fail her somewhat, she had taken to buying old wardrobes, ladies' wardrobes chiefly, which, after mending and renewing, she could sell again to her large circle of customers among the servant-women and mechanics' wives in her neighbourhood. Thus her whole experience of life had been strictly confined to the woman's side of it.

Mrs. Clack was a quiet, small, timid person, who seldom spoke above a faint undertone, as if all she had to say partook of the nature of a secret. Even in her own house she seemed to make herself as small as possible, and to take up as little room as she could. To have a man there, who spoke in a loud and deep voice, and who stretched his legs right across her narrow hearth, blocking up the way to the fire, was the heaviest trial that could have befallen her. She said to herself she would rather have been laid low in sickness.

"It is a cross, a heavy cross!" she murmured between her teeth, as she stood in the farthest corner of the small room, watching old Lister fumbling about the table at the breakfast she had put ready for him. Dot had taken her breakfast sitting comfortably on Mrs. Clack's lap close by the fire, and now she was amusing herself by playing at hide-and-seek amongst the clothed bed-posts of the bed where she had slept as soundly as children sleep, whilst the little woman beside her had lain awake all night fearful of disturbing her if she so much as stirred. But the heavy cross was old Lister, not the little child.

"Ma'am!" he cried, suddenly, so suddenly that her heart began to beat rapidly, and her hands to tremble. "Ma'am, I must visit the Gardens at once. My daughter Hagar will no doubt be seeking me there."

"Yes, sir, yes," she answered, in a nervous tremor.

"I must trouble you to guide me then," he continued.

"Me!" she cried in alarm, "me!"

She could not recollect ever having had to walk beside a man, and to guide one, holding him by the hand, or having his arm in hers, seemed an impossibility. Old Lister had risen as he spoke, and was now groping helplessly about the room in his blindness, looking more than ever in her eyes like some caged wild beast. But there was no one else to give him 'a guiding hand, and she stepped nervously to his aid.

"Dear! dear!" she murmured, "this is a cross."

There was a degree of excitement, however, in the doing of this new and strange service to a man, which was not altogether disagreeable, though she was trembling with agitation. Don was gone out for the whole day, so she was bound to wait upon him herself. But by the time she had brought him his old hat, and his shabby thread-bare overcoat, and found his walking-stick for him, it seemed less impossible for her to guide him down the narrow staircase and through the court into the street, where she trusted to meeting with some boy who, for a few halfpence, would lead him to the Gardens, and bring him back if his daughter should not happen to be there.

There was a lame boy, who went about upon crutches and who was glad enough to take charge of the old man for a small payment, to be paid when he came back. Mrs. Clack kissed little Dot, and shook hands with old Lister, bidding them good-bye, on the chance of never seeing them again; though they were to come in, in time for dinner, if Hagar did not meet with them. It was just such a day as the day before, sunless and foggy; the air was damp and chill, and as the three wayfarers crept along with slow and difficult steps, the cold seemed to wrap them round in an icy mantle. Old Lister was very silent, save that from time to time he asked his guide anxiously if he could not see a tall young woman, with a baby in her arms, looking as if she was searching for somebody. Each time that the lame boy answered "No" he sighed heavily, and for a minute or two pushed on as quickly as the lad's crutches could carry him. Little Dot trotted with short footsteps beside them, patient and quiet, as only young children are who are used to cold and want, and do not know that life has anything better to give them; but even Dot now and then cried softly, and asked if nobody could carry her just a little bit. But how could a blind old man and a boy on crutches bear the burden of a little child?

"My daughter Hagar is bound to be searching for us," said old Lister, again and again, half to himself and half to his guide. He could not give up all hope, though he was fast sinking into despair: his daughter who had been faithful and dutiful to him all her life long, how could she have forsaken him now in his helpless old age? Yet there was a deep and very bitter dread in his inmost heart that she had left him to drift away on the sea of troubles, which had been tossing them to and fro so long.

"Let's tell the police," said the lame guide.

That was still something that could be done, and old Lister snatched at the straw of hope. They stopped every policeman they met, and he told his sad story to each, asking if he had not seen such a person as he described his daughter to be. But his description was misleading, as his blind eyes had never looked into her face and watched the changes time worked upon it. At length, sadly and despondently, he allowed himself, late in the afternoon, to be led back to Mrs. Clack's.

Even Don was astonished to see how Mrs. Clack reconciled herself in a little while to the old man's presence in her house. Dot she delighted in, and she tolerated her grandfather; but it was an extraordinary relief and encouragement to her, as soon as she fairly realised it, to think that he could not see her, or what she was doing. Her nervousness presently passed away, and even his man's voice did not startle her so much after she had heard it for a few days. His blindness put him apart from her almost as if he were occupying another room, except that the sight of his downcast head, drooping on his hands for an hour at a time, and the sound of his heavy sighs, deepening into sobs at times, melted her heart in pity for him. This was not like having a man in the house—a coarse, masterful, domineering man. A poor, blind, forsaken, broken-hearted creature he was, without a friend in the world, and with no hole to creep into for a shelter to his last days. He would nurse Dot on his knee sometimes, but he soon grew tired with her light weight, and his daily though fruitless and painful pilgrimage to the Gardens seemed to wear out all the strength he had.

Mrs. Clack had no fiddle among her stores, as Don had vainly hoped, but by-and-by it came into her mind to buy one which she saw in a pawnbroker's shop, kept by a woman with whom she had long had business dealings, and she brought it home with her in quiet triumph, waiting till all were assembled together in the evening before bringing it out.

"There, sir," she said, in a shrill, pleased voice, as old Lister sat dolefully by the fire, "there's a fiddle for you. It's not many things you crave after, and I'm not a woman to deny everythink to a man. Oh no! A man as never drinks, nor smokes, nor swears is a innocent man, and deserves a fiddle. If you could play, 'Oh, let us be joyful!' maybe I could sing the words; we used to sing it often when I was a girl at school."

Old Lister could not play "Oh, let us be joyful," though Mrs. Clack did her best to hum the tune in a high, cracked key. But he could remember many of the old pieces of music he had once been wont to play in the orchestra of the theatres, and he seemed quite another man with the violin, poor as it was, in his hands. A flush of colour came into the ashy greyness of his face, as his cheek rested fondly against the old instrument. Don beat time joyously with his feet, and Dot danced about the small space round the hearth that was clear of furniture, whilst Mrs. Clack looked on, listening with a beaming face, at the happiness she had created.

"He'll make his fortin'!" cried Don, rapturously, clapping his hard hands till they tingled again, "I said he would! Him, and little Dot, and Cripple Jack must try it on tomorrow; hooray! If you only thought you'd voice and wind enough, Mrs. Clack, you might go along with them; and you'd draw heaps of money, you would. And who knows? You might come across Mrs. Haggar and the baby."

"It 'ud be a sight more likely than going to the Gardings every day," said Mrs. Clack; "you'd be going up and down all the streets, you know, and p'raps she'd hear you or see you, and come running into your arms. But, bless you, Don! I never could lift up my voice in the streets, not to shriek if robbers set upon me! Me, too, that's never sung a hymn since I left school! 'See the leaves around us falling,' and 'Hark! from the tombs a doleful cry!' I recollect them best, but I never sang them after I'd left school." They'd be very nice now, I daresay, but I'd have liked something cheerfuller then."

Next morning Don conducted old Lister, Dot, in a red cloak found among Mrs. Clack's stores, and the boy on crutches, to the streets which he considered most likely to prove a mine of money to the blind fiddler; and after watching them start at a crawl down the middle of the road, with the twanging of the violin-strings calling folks to their windows and doors, he turned away reluctantly to his own field of work.

But fiddling in the streets did not turn out the high road to fortune which Don expected. Some days old Lister managed to bring home a few pence over and above what he had to pay Cripple Jack for his guidance. But more often he came back wet through and chilled to the bone, with not enough to buy a small loaf of bread to eke out Mrs. Clack's tea. The little woman never uttered a word of disappointment, though she felt more keenly than ever how great a failure a man is. She knew she could earn something, if not enough for them all, and Don gave up every penny he could scrape together towards keeping his unfortunate foundlings. If the worst came to the worst, she must break into her little hoard of savings, which she had laid by to keep herself out of the workhouse, as soon as that inevitable day came when she could no longer carry her old-clothes bag up and down the area steps of her usual patrons.

Chapter VII

Old Lister's New Suit

Day after day the faint hope in old Lister's heart that he should find his daughter again smouldered lower and lower. Had she forsaken him and Dot on purpose, out of sheer wickedness and unnaturalness? Or was it partly his own fault for quitting the Gardens before she had had time to return to them? He could not tell, but the result was the same. Here he was dependent upon a strange person, who kept him out of charity, but who would be compelled by-and-by to send him to that dreaded lot which had been hanging over him so long, the ending of his days in the workhouse.

It had never been Mrs. Clack's custom to buy much cast-off masculine attire, and she had only done so under compulsion, when the people she dealt with insisted upon her taking all they had to sell. But now she had a man dependent upon her she looked at it with a more willing eye, examined it more carefully, and offered a more liberal price for it. Old Lister had no clothing but what he was wearing when Don found him; and this was very worn and thin. It seemed to be in the very nick of time that a whole suit was offered to her as a great bargain, not very much the worse for wear, and one that had fitted a man pretty much the same size as old Lister. Mrs. Clack bought them so cheaply that she, came home in great triumph, although she was bent double under the weight of her blue linen clothes-bag.

"There, sir!" she exclaimed, "I've got a bargain for you. That's a real gentleman's suit, that is. I daresay when Don comes in he'll be proud to help you to dress yourself up in 'em, so as I can see where they fit, and where they don't fit. There's a top coat for you—feel it; double-breasted and velvet collar and cuffs, scarcely the worse for wear, and other garments, as it's a thousand pities you haven't the eyes to see how new and fresh they look, not gone at the knees at all; and a strong, stout cloth that you can feel how good it is. You'd be took more notice of in the streets with that suit on. Folks 'ud take you for a gentleman come down in the world; as no doubt you are, sir. I'm hoping Don mayn't be too late to-night."

Fortunately, Don came in earlier than usual, and old Lister, as pleased as a child with his new suit, withdrew into the coach-house below where he and Don slept. Mrs. Clack clapped her hands with delight and admiration when he re-appeared.

"I shouldn't have known you again, sir," she cried. "Now I've a real pleasure in looking at you. I could never ha' thought that the sight of any man could ha' given me so much pleasure. Yes, you'll do wonders now; folks could never pass by and overlook you in that suit, I know. And if it was only summer; instead of being February, and bitter cold, we'd all take a little trip down the river as far as Greenwich, with your fiddle, and see what luck we had. I never made such a good bargain before, and I wish you luck and long life to enjoy your new suit, sir."

"I wish my daughter Hagar could see me," said the old man, half proudly, whilst he stroked the velvet cuffs and collar of his new coat, with a pleased and lingering touch.

He felt warm and comfortable in it the next day, as he slowly paced the streets, though time wind was blowing from the east, and numbed his fingers, and made him draw very, very wailing notes from his violin-strings. Passers-by took more notice of him than they had done in his threadbare and beggarly garb; and more money was given to him, even two or three sixpences in silver, as though Mrs. Clack's foresight was true, and people really took him for a gentleman come down in the world. He had never carried home half so much money, and when he put it down on Mrs. Clack's little table, and listened to the clinking of it as she counted it up, his sad old heart felt cheered as it had not done since he had lost his daughter Hagar.

"It is every farthing your due, ma'am," he said to Mrs. Clack, as she pushed it back against his hand, which rested on the table. "We've been living on your charity all this while: and I've often considered it was possibly my duty to hide my head, and my grandchild's head, in the dreaded union. But hope is coming back to me, ma'am; hope with her silver wings. Take the money, Mrs. Clack; every farthing of it is your own."

"It's very beautiful to hear you talk so, sir," she answered, with tears in her eyes; "but a man ought always to have a little in his pockets, for other folks to see he's not without a penny. It's not the same with women; nobody expects us to have our pockets full; they may be as empty as empty. The more I dwell on it, the more difference I see betwixt men and women. Certainly it's a wonderful mystery; only we've both got human hearts, and you'd not see me die of want, I'm sure; and it 'ud be a comfort to me to know wherever you are you'd got a few pence by you in case o' need."

But a day or two after this, when Don woke one morning in the dark coach-house, and struck a match to light their farthing candle, old Lister's white head was tossing to and fro in an uneasy slumber, and he was moaning pitifully in his sleep. The bed on which they both lay was nothing but a thin flock mattress, stretched on a heap of straw and rags to keep it from the damp of the ground. The place was choked up with Mrs. Clack's stores; cast-off clothing of all kinds, and of all sizes. The air was close and heavy with the unwholesome smell of apparel that had been worn and laid aside unwashed. There was little light, and no ventilation in this old coach*house, and the feeble glimmer of the candle hardly lit up the corner where the mattress lay.

"I'm very ill," moaned old Lister, opening his sightless eyes at the sound of the match being struck; "tell Mrs. Clack I can't go out to-day. I cannot lift up my old head."

As the day wore on there was no doubt that he was very ill, and when Don came home again at night, Mrs. Clack sent him at once for the nearest doctor, who lived at the corner of the next street, and was not above keeping a shop, and mixing up medicines from the prescriptions of more skilful and more lucky physicians. When he came he found Mrs. Clack seated disconsolately by the side of the old man, whilst Dot was on the bed, kissing and fondling him, though he would not stir or take any notice of her. The doctor gazed long and studiously at the feverish, wrinkled face, and felt the burning hand and quickly-beating pulse.

"He's half famished," he said, "and he's down with fever. And no wonder," he added, glancing round him, and breathing the close, tainted air with an expression of disgust; "it's dens like these that breed fever. You're his wife, I suppose?"

"No! oh, dear, no!" she cried, nervously; "I'll not deceive you, sir; I'm nobody's wife. But I'll do my duty by him as much as if I was. Tell me what I ought to do and I'll do it. Did you say it was fever, doctor?"

"It's fever, sure enough," he answered, hastening to the door for a breath of fresh air.

"It couldn't be that suit!" exclaimed Mrs. Clack, clasping her hands. "I've never dealt in fever clothes or small-pox clothes, I 'haven't indeed, sir. But I'd a suit of clothes offered to me very cheap only a day or two ago; and he's been wearing them. Oh, doctor, it couldn't be that suit?"

"Very likely," he replied, "if it was a great bargain; and whoever sold them to you is guilty of murder, for he'll die, poor old fellow. There isn't a chance for him. Half- starved to begin with," he muttered to himself, "and breathing air that's full of poison."

In a few hours all the neighbours knew that the blind old fiddler was down with fever, and that he was raving and rambling in his talk, not with any violence, his aged worn-out frame had not strength enough for that, but with cries, and moans, and loud words, which could easily be overheard on the outside of the coach-house doors. Women and children clustered round listening, in spite of Don, who rushed out from time to time, unexpectedly, with as little noise as possible, to drive them away. "It was a dreadful catching fever," they told one another; but none of them seemed afraid of taking it. Some of the oldest neighbours proffered their help to Mrs. Clack; but she would never leave the old man, except when Don was at home to take her place.

The fever was not very long in finishing its work on a frame so feeble as old Lister's. His mind grew somewhat clearer towards the end, though he was almost too far gone to speak.

"Tell me," he said, with his failing voice, seeing no face, and not knowing who was near him; "tell me, any one, where I am going?"

Don was kneeling on the floor beside him, and Dot was lying near him on the mattress, watching him with her wondering childish eyes, whilst Mrs. Clack sat by him on a low stool, bathing his hot head with vinegar. None of them spoke, though Don looked up eagerly into Mrs. Clack's face.

I'm going," he said mournfully; "where to?"

"Oh, Mrs. Clack," said Don, in a low, appealing voice; "you're a wise woman; couldn't you tell him nothink about where he's going to?"

"I've forgotten it, Don," she answered, sadly; "it's so long since I learned it."

"I'm dying like a dog at last," muttered old Lister, turning his blind eyes from side to side, as if vainly strving to see something.

"Oh no, no!" cried Don, earnestly; "you can't do that; there's those of us by you as loves you, and is very sorry for you. There's Mrs. Clack, and Dot, and me. Isn't there nobody to love him where he is going to, Mrs. Clack?"

"Yes," she said, solemnly, "there's God—"

"God is where you are going to," said Don, in the old man's ear, "and He loves you."

"And our Lord Jesus Christ," continued Mrs. Clack, slowly, as if she was half afraid of uttering His name.

"And Jesus Christ," repeated Don. "There's me, and Dot, and Mrs. Clack here as loves you, and is taking care of you; and there's God and Jesus Christ where you are going to, as loves you, and is taking care of you. That's not dying like a dog!"

A strange and solemn expression passed over the old man's dying face. He looked as if he was listening to some good news long ago forgotten, but now told to him again. His lips moved; but only Don caught the whisper that they uttered:

God be merciful to me, a sinner!"

Chapter VIII

The Cares of this Life

In the evening of old Lister's funeral Mrs. Clack sat alone and idle at her fireside. She had no heart to set to work on the mending and refurbishing the cast-off clothes about her. It was a real grief of mind to her that the only man she had ever had to do with should have been buried in a pauper's grave; but she could not prudently afford to give him any other burial. Her hoard of savings was small and her stock had been seriously damaged by the rough mode of disinfecting it which had been gone through as soon as the worn-out body of the blind old man had been carried away to the dead-house. Poor Don was down with the fever, and had been sent off immediately by the doctor to the fever hospital. No one but herself and Dot had been left to follow the old man's coffin: and little Dot had enjoyed the trip to the cemetery. She was gone to play with some neighbour's children now; and Mrs. Clack sat, tearful and down-hearted, by her solitary fire.

What made it seem so solitary? For many a long year she had lived alone, and no face had met her eyes when she looked round her little room, and no voice had fallen on her ear. She had chosen to live alone, priding herself upon keeping aloof from the fellow-creatures among whom her lot had been cast. She was one who kept herself to herself, was her boast. What good came of gossiping and neighbouring? As long as she could take care of herself she would be beholden to nobody; and nobody had any claim upon her. So for many years she had lived alone; and people had died, and children had been born into the world, and sorrow and sickness had befallen her neighbours living thickly around her, and joy and gladness had shone upon their homes for a brief season, and she had neither wept with them, nor rejoiced with them. Why should she feel solitary and sad now?

It was Don that had done it. She could remember how the lonely, homeless boy, when he was a little lad of ten, had met her one day bending and staggering under an unusually heavy load, and how he had insisted upon hoisting it on his own little shoulders, and tottering beneath it till he reached her door. From that day to this he had made himself so useful to her, that it was but a small return to let him sleep at night on the old mattress in the room below. He had seldom taken a piece of bread from her, but had picked up his own living she hardly knew how; only turning in for shelter each night, and serving her as if he could not do enough to repay her. What had she done for Don? What trouble had she taken for him? She, who had been well-taught in her youth, who could read and write better than nineteen out of every twenty folks like them, what had she taught Don? For nearly four years he had attached himself to her, and he knew nothing yet of God, nothing of any life beyond this; nothing of Jesus Christ and His death upon the cross. He was as dark and ignorant as when she first knew him.

Suppose Don died in the fever hospital! He might as well have lived in a heathen land, for all he knew about death and what comes after death. The heathen knew more than he did, for they had gods, and prayed to them, though they were false ones. But Don had no knowledge of any god. Why had she never taught him?

The tears stole slowly down Mrs. Clack's cheeks. She knew about God and His Son Jesus Christ. All the wondrous story of God's love to the world had been familiar to her in her girlhood; she could have answered any question about the life of Jesus Christ. Somewhere she had a Bible that had been given to her as a reward for her Scripture knowledge. But she had lost all thought of such things; she had forgotten them altogether. The many cares of this world, and the hard struggle for a livelihood had choked the good seed sown in her childhood. It was many a long year now since she had given a single thought to her Father in heaven, or to her Saviour who had lived on earth a life of toil and care like her own.

Then as she sat there, sad and lonely, she seemed in her own mind almost to see Jesus Christ, in all His goodness and holiness, passing His time, not in solitude like herself selfishly holding Himself aloof from the rough, ignorant people about Him, but dwelling like a neighbour in the midst of them; walking with them in the fields; sitting with them in the house; rowing out with them in their boats; feasting with them; going to their funerals; being so pressed by them that He could scarcely make His way along the streets and lanes. Did Jesus never hear the neighbours gossiping? Did nobody run to tell Him when a baby was born in the same street? or when two young folks were going to be married? And did He turn a deaf ear to all this common news, and pass by as if it had nothing to do with Him?

Her own heart answered that the Lord Jesus Christ, the Son of God, must have led a very different life from hers, or He could never have been the Saviour of men. Why! she had saved no one, not even saved them a few minutes' trouble. Jesus had borne their sins, sorrows, and sicknesses; but she had done nothing, until Don had brought old Lister and little Dot to her door; and her heart, thank God, had not been hard enough to turn them away to starve. But that was Don's doing; and, oh, she was glad she had taken them in, and borne with them, and learned to love them a little. She fell down on her knees, and hid her tearful face in her hands, praying to God to pardon her long forgetfulness of His love, and to help her to live no longer to herself. It was a long time before she rose from her knees. She was not praying so much as remembering what Jesus Christ had done for her; His love and sorrow that had been so sinfully neglected by her all these years. What He required of her to do was to go out amongst her fellow creatures, and follow in His steps. It would be a great trial, but she must do it.

When Don came back she would teach him diligently all she knew. She had seen poor old Lister die in gloom and darkness, when she ought to have been ready with a blessed light to shine upon his way to the grave. Dying like a dog. Yes, it would be dying like a dog, if there was no Father in heaven, and no home there to go to.

It would be worse than that, for a dog dies with no thought of such a thing, with no longing wish to go home to God, and to feel His love. But to lie dying with that darkness all about one, and think that there might have been hope, and joy, and a blessed entrance into another life, and dear friends' faces smiling a welcome, and Jesus Christ Himself to receive the soul; to think all this might have been, yet was not, would make a man's death a thousand times worse than a dog's.

And this life! What a poor miserable, wretched thing that was, at any rate for poor folks, if this world were all. Toiling, and striving, and scraping, and going without comforts, almost without necessaries, seldom eating quite enough, scarcely ever warm in winter or cool in summer, wearing rags, and walking almost barefoot; if this were all, better a thousand times be a dog than a man or a woman, with a heart to feel for the little children growing up in misery, and for the old people passing out of it in darkness. How was it she could have gone on so long without a thought of God, and the heaven He dwelt in, and the love He felt for the world, when He sent His only son to save it. What a foolish, selfish, sinful woman she had been, all these years!

She was so deep in thought that she hardly heard a low and timid knock at the outer door at the foot of the staircase; but when a second tap came, she opened her window, and looked down into the dark court, where the figure of a girl stood below her.

"Please, Mrs. Clack," said a sorrowful voice, "I'm Peggy Watson, and mother's struck with the fever, and father says p'raps you'd be so good as lend us the loan of the mattress the blind fiddler died on, so as to leave mother by herself. We've only one bed, and she throws herself about so."

"I'll come down myself, and see her, my dear," answered Mrs. Clack.

Here was a call come at once, as if direct from heaven, to prove if she would really follow Christ, who came to give His life for His brethren. She had always passed those people with downcast eyes and averted face, as being lower and more ignorant than herself, but now she made haste to go down quickly to their help.

It was no light task she had undertaken. Peggy was a rough, untaught girl of twelve, and the house, which was the same sort of dwelling as her own, was bare and comfortless. But Mrs. Clack removed her neighbour into her own more comfortable home, and nursed her there until the fever was passed, and she was pronounced out of danger.

"You've saved my life, Mrs. Clack," said Mrs. Watson, faintly, one day; "but if it weren't for the poor children I'd as lief have gone. There's nought worth livin' for as I can see, and nothin' worth dyin' for, but any how it's over when one's in the grave-yard."

"Hush! hush!" she answered. "There's Jesus Christ to live for, ay, and to die for. I've thought so many a time whilst you've been ill."

Her voice trembled a little as she said it, but she called up all her courage, and the woman's sunken eyes turned to her with an eager gaze.

"I've heard a little of Him," she said, "but I hardly know anything. There's my brother wrote me a good letter once about Him you spoke of, but I couldn't make much of it. You're a scholar, and may be you'd write to Jem, and tell him I've been down with fever, and p'raps he'd have me over for a bit, when I'm well enough to go. I'm almost dyin' for a breath o' country air."

"I'll write," said Mrs. Clack, cheerfully. She felt shy yet at speaking openly to any one of the change that had passed over her own soul, and it seemed easier to her to do something for her neighbour. She wrote the letter, and a speedy answer came, enclosing a few shillings, to pay the sick woman's fare to Reading, and inviting Mrs. Clack to accompany her. Mrs. Watson was yet so weak, that she begged of her to go with her, and take a holiday for a few days.

"Little Dot can stay with our children," she urged; "Peggy's that fond of her nobody could tell, and you'd be all the better for a rest and a mouthful of fresh air. Oh, Mrs. Clack, you've been so good to me, you never could leave me to go alone. And you and my good brother 'ud be such friends! He goes preachin' on Sundays, though he's a poor man, and never got much learnin' when he was a lad. May be he'll show me whether there's anything worth livin' for."

"But who'll take care of Don if he comes back while I'm away?" asked Mrs. Clack.

"Peggy will take care of Don," she answered, "if he gets out of hospital while we're away, but we shan't be more than a week, and if ever I'm strong enough to do some charing again, I'll pay you back your expenses. Only say you'll come."

It would be a great treat to her, a wonderful treat to see the country again after so many years of London streets and London smoke. Dot was quite at home with the children and Peggy, and Don might not be back for a fortnight. So a few days after the invitation Mrs. Clack, and her neighbour, white-faced, and worn to a shadow, stood side by side on the platform of Paddington Station, looking in bewilderment and dismay at the confusion around them. Mrs. Clack's heart failed her, and a nervous trembling seized upon her, which made every object swim and dance before her eyes, when a pleasant voice speaking to her gave her a faint hope.

"Where is it you want to go to?" asked the guard.

"Oh, to Reading, please," she said, timidly, looking up into the face of a tall man, who was smiling down upon her.

"Now, don't put yourself about," he said, kindly, "I'm the guard of this train, and I'll put you into a carriage, and see you out again at the right place. You're not used to travelling? Never mind, I'll take as much care of you as if you were as precious as china. And you are more precious than china," he added, smiling again at her flurried face.

"You are very good, sir," she answered, tremulously, "and oh, if we could but come back with you. We're going into the country beyond Reading for a week, me and my neighbour; and we haven't been on the railway for years. If we could only come by your train."

"Well," he said, "whenever you're on this line you ask at the station for Abbott, they all know me, and if I'm anywhere about I'll see after you. I shall be coming back to London, Mondays, Wednesdays, and Fridays, next week. I'll write it down for you and the time of the train, and you look out for me at Reading if you return either of those days. You'll remember me?"

Ay! I shall remember you, sir, and God bless you!" said Mrs. Clack.

Chapter IX

A Troubled Conscience

Hagar remained in the hospital until she began to feel as if it was her home, so long she lay there in the same bed, seeing the same faces from day to day. That there was no other home for her made her cling more to this hospital ward, and dread the day when she would be well enough to be dismissed. But in spite of her dread, and of her homelessness, the time came when she was pronounced cured; and though she was still unfit to face the cold world again, alone and feeble, it was necessary for her to make way for another yet more helpless than herself if there was no other place to go to, the workhouse was always open to her.

Hagar hardly cared what became of her; the bitter despair and weariness of life that possessed her when she abandoned her father and her little girl, were not yet cast out of her soul. Remorse was blended with her despair now, for day and night the picture of her blind old father and the helpless child as she had seen them last, was present to her mind. It was this which made her recovery so slow: outwardly she was silent and submissive, always obeying her nurse and the doctor, but inwardly she was fretting and chafing herself with tormenting thoughts.

At length the day came when she must go; her own tattered clothing was brought to her, made to look as clean and respectable as it could be, yet she dressed herself in it silently, hating the very sight and touch of these rags, which seemed a badge of her utter poverty and friendlessness. What could there be before her but to wander about the streets, hiding her head anywhere she could for a shelter, and dying in some hole at last, uncared for and unknown? A fitting end for one like her, she said to herself.

Abbott left a message for you yesterday," said the nurse to her, when she was ready to go; "if you've nowhere else you want to go to, we're to send you in a cab to the house where he lives, and he'll be at home tonight. His cousin, who is a dressmaker, lives at the same place, and will be there to take you in."

Hagar lifted up her drooping head, and the almost sullen gloom of her face brightened a little. Abbott's messages to her had been the only link between her and the outer world, and had brought the only gleam of hope to her dark mind. She had seen him once, and his face had been the face of a friend. He had told her, too, that the same coffin held his mother and her baby; and it seemed as if this formed some kind of kinship between them.

Very bitterly and sadly she looked out on the busy streets as she drove through them in the cab, until the high naked branches of the trees in Kensington Gardens came into sight, and there rushed upon her more keenly than ever the recollection of that dreadful day in November. She would have given the world to bring that time back again, and meet once more the trouble and the difficulty from which she had fled then. She knew now that it would have been better to have suffered death than to have fled from her duty. It was cowardly and cruel to forsake those two helpless creatures, so closely bound to her. God had bound them to her; she had received life from one, and given life to the other. Yet she had forsaken them, and what could she answer when she was called to judgment, and God asked her what had become of them?

She had not recovered from the terror of her own thoughts when she reached the house where Abbott lived. His cousin the dressmaker was expecting her, and received her with a pleasant heartiness, as if she were some welcome visitor. She led her up to a little room in the attic, where a fire was burning brightly in a tiny grate, and tea was laid out on a little spindle-legged table, beside which stood a comfortable, warmly-padded, old-fashioned chair for her to rest in. There was a wide and cheerful view from the high window, looking over a few roofs across to green fields, and a sky-line broken by trees to the west. Hagar had seldom looked out on so great a space of sky, which was already flecked with early sunset clouds, and she stood at the window gazing out at it, whilst the dressmaker lingered a few minutes, pouring boiling water on the tea, and looking about to see if there was anything lacking for Hagar's comfort.

"I have no time to spare," she said, kindly, "or I would stay while you get your tea; but my cousin Abbott asked me to make you welcome. He has told me all he knows about you, and I'm sure you'll find him and me ready to be your friends. I laid that little baby of yours beside my good old cousin in her coffin; and, my dear, my heart bleeds for you. There now! Don't. you cry; come and take your tea while it's hot and refreshing."

Hagar could not speak for weeping. This was so like coming home, and yet it was not coming home! Abbott knew nothing about her, and her great sin, and when he did could not he, and this good, kindly woman shrink with horror from her? A true, strong, good man like him could never understand her despair, or forgive her for yielding to it. And, oh! where were they now, her father and little Dot? Whilst she was surrounded with all this comfort and kindness, perhaps they were starving with cold and hunger, if they were not already at rest in their graves. The comfort was unbearable to her; she fancied she would have been almost happier wandering footsore and hungry about the streets. The first time she saw Abbott she must tell him all, and bear any consequences that might arise from her confession.

Abbott came up to see her that evening. As soon as she heard his tap at the door, she rose and stood trembling before him in her poor tattered clothing, and with her white and sickly face meeting him with a look of trouble and affright. He had only seen her once before, for he had not been admitted to visit her a second time at the hospital after he had thrown her back by his conversation. He had never beheld a more pitiable creature, for her long illness and the great anguish of her soul had marked her face with an expression of profound suffering.

"Sit down," he said, gently; "you're not fit to be standing."

"I've something to say to you," she stammered; "something I ought to tell you, for I don't deserve what you are doing for me."

"Let us sit down and talk it over," he answered, drawing the only other chair to the opposite side of the narrow hearth. "Tell me anything you wish."

"I was very miserable," said Hagar, clasping her thin hands together, "and I lost all heart. My husband was dead, and there was my blind father, and my two little children, all looking to me for everything. I'd done the best I could, but I couldn't get a living for us all; and my poor father would never hear a word of going into the workhouse. We'd seen better days, you know, and he couldn't bring his mind to it—no, if we were all starved to death. He kept on saying he'd die like a dog first, and so I grew quite desperate."

"Did you ask God to help you? Did you try to cast your cares upon Him?" said Abbott, as she paused, afraid and ashamed of saying more.

"I never thought of Him," she answered. "I never thought of Him when we were well off and happy, and it's hard to remember Him when you haven't a morsel, and two little children and an old man all crying to you from hunger. I'd forgotten God, and He forgot me. If He hadn't forsaken me then, He must have forsaken me now."

"Men forsake us," said Abbott, "but God never."

"Ay! you don't know," continued Hagar, with dry lips and in a forced voice; "I took my old blind father, and my little, little Dot—only this high—into Kensington Gardens, and I forsook them, I'd no roof to shelter them, and no bread to give them, and I grew tired to death, and I forsook them both."

"Poor mother!" cried Abbott, "oh, if I'd only been there!"

He felt, as he had often felt before when he heard some tale of misery, that if he had been there he must have saved them. They were silent for a minute or two, Hagar gazing with dry tearless eyes into the fire, not daring to look into his face, which was full of grief and pity and sympathy for her sore distress.

"I don't deserve to be here," she cried, glancing round the little room; "I ought to be out in the cold night and under the dark, wet trees, as I left them. But I did go back to find them, only it was too late. I climbed up into the Gardens after the gates were closed, and walked about all night, up and down, calling. And then I was knocked down and my baby killed. I'm left quite alone now. That is God's judgment on me."

"You would not do it again," he said.

"I'd rather die a hundred times," she sobbed; "there's many and many a thing worse than dying. I never knew misery like this. To have your own heart crying out against you all the while, and to wonder, and to wonder where they are, and think what dreadful things may have come upon them and me not to know—that is misery?'

"If you'd only speak to our Lord Jesus Christ and tell Him all about it," said Abbott, in a low and troubled voice: "just speak as if you could see Him, and ask Him to forgive you, and if He thinks best to let you find them again,—you'd feel your misery lighter, I'm sure. 'Come unto Me,' He says, 'all ye that labour and are heavy laden, and I will give you rest.' And you are weary and heavy laden. He feels for you, and is troubled for you, just as I am, only a hundred times more. There is nothing like going to Him."

"I don't know what words to say," she answered; "I never said any prayer but 'Our Father!' and not that often. Will you speak to Him for me.

"Now?" he asked.

"Yes," she said; "if anything 'ud comfort me it's that. You're a good man, and God will listen to you. Perhaps He'll listen to me some time, but I can't feel as if He'd hear me now. You pray to Him for me, so that I can join in."

"Dear Lord!" said Abbott; "we know Thou'rt always going up and down London streets, seeing every sin, and every trouble in them. Thou'rt a man of sorrows and acquainted with grief still, O Lord. When this poor woman forsook her father and her little child, it was done in Thy sight; Thou wert standing by, and you hast had them in Thy sight ever since. They can not be lost, or hidden from Thee. O Lord, forgive the poor mother's sin. She's in great trouble; I never saw any one in so much trouble! Don't let her feel herself forsaken by God; that's an awful thing, dear Lord! She is very weary and heavy laden, oh, give her rest. Forgive her, and comfort her; and in some good time let her find her father and child again. Amen."

"Do you think He will bring them back to me?" asked Hagar, feverishly, after they had risen from their knees.

"I can't tell," answered Abbott; "if it is good for you, and for them, He will. But none of us can know what God thinks best."

"Oh!", she cried, "I shall never believe He has forgiven me, and hasn't forsaken me if He doesn't bring them back to me.".

"Now you judge God to be like yourself" he said, gravely, "because you forsook them you think He will forsake you. But His ways are not our ways, nor His thoughts our thoughts. Your love was worn out by your misery, but His love can never be worn out."

He said no more, but bade her good night, and left her in her quiet room. Hagar, exhausted, yet too excited for sleep, sat watching the fire till the last spark was dead, pondering in her heart what she must do to gain some news of her lost ones, if possible, and repeating to herself from time to time the words "God's love can never be worn out."

Chapter X

There was no difficulty in finding work for Hagar. She had always been quick and clever with her needle, and Abbott's cousin was glad enough to employ her. Her work was done in her own room at first, because her clothes were too poor for her to join the other dressmakers in the work room below; and afterwards by her own choice, for she was still too sick at heart to bear the common chit-chat of the work-room. It was very quiet and still up there under the roof; and she had time enough for brooding thoughts as her busy fingers stitched away from hour to hour. She had more comfort and leisure than she ever remembered in her life, for when her husband was alive, and her father a musician at the theatres, they had spent their income recklessly, with no thought of the future and its possible calamities; and very often she had spent their last shilling in utter uncertainty as to where the next would come from. She could not keep herself from dwelling upon that now, and reckoning up the foolish and extravagant waste of money which might have saved her from the extreme straits she had fallen into.

She was learning eagerly what Abbott had to tell her of the love of God, and of Jesus Christ, whom He has sent. Abbott spoke with the certainty of one who knew what he was saying. God was no dread Being far away in some distant heaven; nor was Christ an absent Saviour dwelling in a marvellous and unapproachable glory. He told her what he himself felt of the constant and abiding sense of the presence of God with him, and she listened, almost afraid of having the same feeling. As yet it was only as a lesson learned by the memory; she could not give herself up to it, and receive it into her very heart. The long night of her despair was not quite ended, and it seemed to her as if the day could never dawn, unless she heard something of her lost ones. Abbott sympathised so fully in this feeling of Hagar's, that he could not himself be at rest concerning her old father and little Dot. He set on foot inquiries after them wherever he thought there was a chance of their being traced. The policemen in Kensington Gardens recollected having seen a blind old man and a little girl, led by a cripple on crutches, who had been seeking for some one a few weeks before Christmas, but they had not been seen for a long while. Abbott spent his spare time in going from workhouse to workhouse, and from refuge to refuge, often taking half the night for his search, yet he was unable to find any clue to their fate. More than once, after hearing a vague rumour of a blind fiddler, he travelled to the farthest end of London, only to find himself disappointed, and to make Hagar still more heart-sick with baffled hope.

Once, if she had but known it, old Lister and little Dot crept slowly along the very street where she was living, but her garret window opened to the back of the house, and though she caught the distant notes of a violin, the sound was too frequent to arouse her attention, especially as her father's old fiddle had been broken months ago. She only thought of him and sighed heavily. Scarcely an hour passed by when she did not only mourn and sigh over the unknown lot of him and her little child. If she had but seen them die, and had closed their eyes, and laid their heads in the coffin, she thought she could be at rest. But what were they doing? Where were they dwelling? When the bitter east winds of March whistled past her attic-window, and the sleet fell aslant on the roofs, drifting into every little niche where the sparrows were shivering, and when the darkness of the night stole over the crowded mazes of the city, she wondered, with an aching heart, where her father's grey head and her child's tender limbs were sheltering. Oh, if they should be without shelter such nights as these, hiding under an archway, or crouching down on some doorstep! It would be better to know that they had found the refuge of the grave.

But the whole month of March was not wild and wintry. The week that Mrs. Clack was spending in the country was a fine and sunny one, with a few April showers falling before their time. The leaf-buds in the hedgerows opened their fresh young green, and some daisies peeped out where snow had been lying only a few days before. The brown brooks were full of swirling, chattering streams, and the birds, busier than they had been since last spring, were flitting from tree to tree seeking house-room for their nests. Mrs. Clack had been so long in London that she felt herself in a new world. She had not watched lambs at play since she was a school-girl, and her heart throbbed almost painfully when she first caught sight of them. To many an eye, over-wearied with sight-seeing, there was nothing very beautiful in the quiet country scenery about her, but to her every common thing she saw was full of pleasure, and she could hardly believe she was herself the same woman who was used to trudging wearily along the hard pavements, and up and down area-steps, burdened with her bag of cast-off clothes.

But the week came to an end, and though Mrs. Watson was going to stay longer, Mrs. Clack felt bound to return: to her neglected business, as well as to little Dot and her own home. She carried with her a tolerably heavy basket of country fare: fresh eggs, gathered from the nest by her own hand, butter just churned, and some early vegetables, such as she had seldom tasted. She was right glad to be seen and hailed by Abbott, on the Reading platform, for she had taken care to return by his train, and he found her a seat, and lifted her basket in for her—just as if she had been a lady, she said to herself. It was not a long journey, for the train only stopped once for taking the tickets; but in the crush and hurry at Paddington Station Abbott sought out the timid old woman, who was looking scared to death at the confusion about her.

"I knew you'd be frightened," he said, lifting out her basket; "my mother was always scared at this station, so I waited a minute to look after you, or generally I'm off like a shot. Which way do you go home? and how do you mean to go?"

"I live in Chelsea, sir," answered Mrs. Clack, "and I can walk home very well through Kensington Gardings."

"That's partly my way, at least as far as the Gardens," said Abbott: "so I can carry your basket as far as we go together. It's pounds too heavy for you."

"If you'd only take an egg or two by way of return," cried Mrs. Clack, quite overcome by his kindness,—"they're real country eggs, laid by country hens, as you're wife 'ud relish ever so, I'm sure."

"I'm not married," said Abbott, looking down at her flushed old face with a smile.

"Dear! dear!" exclaimed Mrs. Clack. They had turned into the streets, and the rattle of wheels and tramp of horses about them made her feel as if she could not make her new friend hear her feeble voice. She glanced up at him in silent admiration, nodding, and smiling whenever she met his eye, and putting out her utmost strength to keep pace with him. It was a marvel that such a man should not be married.

When they reached Kensington Gardens, Abbott hesitated a few seconds, balancing the basket in his strong hand, and looking down at Mrs. Clack's small spare figure.

"About as little as my mother," he muttered. "I'll step across the Gardens with you," he added, aloud, "it's many a month since I've been here, and it will be quite a treat. I used to come sometimes with my mother."

"And she's dead?" remarked Mrs. Clack, with timid pity.

"Yes," he answered.

"Dear! dear!" she said, "it 'ud be a bitter trouble to her to leave a son like you. I never knew anything of men, except quite the outside, till lately, and now those I come across seem as good as good! I've just been visiting a good man down in the country; and it all comes of Don picking up a blind old man and a little girl in these very Gardings, and bringing them home to me. I said I'd rather have ten dogs than a man; but I didn't know what a blessing a man could be."

"A blind old' man, and a little girl!" cried Abbott; "not old John Lister and little Dot!"

"Why, you know them!" exclaimed Mrs. Clack, her face beaming with surprise and delight. "Ay, Don found them here last November; a dreary night it was. Don is my errand boy, and sleeps on the premises, and he brought them home to me. And the little girl does answer to the name of Dot, which isn't her chrissen name, I'm sure. The old man had been left by his daughter in the Gardings; he didn't know whether it was a purpose or not"

"Thank God!" said Abbott, standing still in the path, and lifting his hat from his head.

"You know them?" continued Mrs. Clack.

"I know Hagar," he answered, "and she's breaking her heart after them. Thank God I came with you, and did not leave you before you told me this! Where are they? in your house still?"

"The poor blind old man's dead and buried," she answered, bursting into tears. "I bought him a fine new suit of clothes, a great bargain, and it was a fever suit as I knew nothing about; and he took the fever badly, and died. Oh! I wish I'd never done it! It were that as killed him; and he'd have been so happy now. He was always mourning for his daughter Hagar."

"Poor Hagar!" said Abbott, in a low tone. It would be a bitter grief to her, he knew; and his heart ached for her. She had been cherishing a hope of finding her father and Dot again, as a sign that God had forgiven her: and he could not persuade her to trust in God's love and pardon without a sign.

"But there is Dot," he added, after a pause.

"Oh yes! she's all right and well," replied Mrs. Clack, "I left her with my neighbour's daughter, Peggy Watson. I'd been nursing Mrs. Watson through the fever she caught from poor old Mr. Lister, and she would not have nay, but I must go down into the country with her. I'd been nursing the old man before that, and never did I think a man could be such a harmless creature. He lived with me three months, and never said a miss word; never."

"I must come home with you," said Abbott, "and we will take poor Dot to her mother at once, this very night. She is almost broken-hearted, poor thing!"

It was quite dark in the narrow mews as they passed into it, for the single lamp in the midst of it had not been lit, as the glass had been broken the day before. Mrs. Clack knew her way perfectly in the dark, but

Abbott stumbled over the uneven pavement as he followed her. At the farther end a dim gleam of candle-light shone faintly through a dusty window in the Watsons' dwelling-place, where Dot was to be found. They made their way towards it; and Mrs. Clack knocked hurriedly at the door. The casement overhead was opened, and Peggy craned over her dirty face, and rough, untidy head to see who was below.

"I'm Mrs. Clack come home," she said, "and I want Dot."

"Oh, Mrs. Clack," she cried, "we lost Dot yesterday; and she's not been heard of again yet. None of the p'leece has seen her."

Chapter XI

Bad News for Don

Don had been sent down from the fever hospital to a Convalescent Home at the sea-side for a week or two, till he could return to his life in London strong enough to have some hope of recovering his former health. He had not written to Mrs. Clack, because he could not write, and had only taken his first lessons in that useful art in the home ho had just left; but the mother at the Home had written a letter to her, and guided his hand whilst he signed his name to it; and he was very proud of his new accomplishment. But he was not troubled with any doubts of Mrs. Clack's giving him a welcome when he returned to his old haunts. He felt as certain that she would be overjoyed to see him again, as he could he to see her. Whole years seemed to have passed over him since the day old Lister had died, and he had sunk under the fever himself. He had grown a good deal during his illness, and his old clothes were uncomfortably short in the arms and legs, though he had chosen them much too large, to give him plenty of room to grow in. But he could trust Mrs. Clack and her wisdom to set this little difficulty right.

He had a thousand strange things to tell her; especially of the wonderful sights to be seen on the seashore; and the marvellous stories he had heard of that same Lord Jesus Christ, whose name she had spoken to the poor blind man as he lay dying. He could not believe that Mrs. Clack knew all those beautiful stories; or surely she would have told them to him long ago. For they were true; that was the chief beauty of them. The mother at the Convalescent Home had read them to him out of a book, as he lay on the sea-shore; and had even taught him to read a few words to himself. He had brought a little book of texts back with him; and he would ask Mrs. Clack to hear him read every night, till he knew every word, and could read them to himself or to any poor creature that lay a-dying, not knowing where they were going to, or what Jesus Christ had done for their sakes. His heart was very full when he turned into the mews once more. He was ready to cry with joy; and a few tears actually escaped from under his eyelids, to be brushed away quickly, lest anybody should see them. He was going to sit down in his old seat by Mrs. Clack's fire, with little Dot on his knee, and Mrs. Clack in her rocking-chair opposite to them, listening to all his wonderful news. He had learned how to sing "Oh! let us be joyful!" and now he and Mrs. Clack and Dot could all sing it together.

It was dusk, the very how of his usual return; and he knocked his one single quiet tap at Mrs. Clack's door. There was no answer. After a while he knocked a second time, and stepped back to look up at the window. There was no light. That was not unusual, for he knew she loved to sit in the twilight; but there was a white blind across the window; and there was a strange stillness, and a sense of emptiness about the closed house, which struck him forcibly. He tried the latch, but that was fast; and though he knocked a third time, no notice was taken of him.

Don sat down on the low door sill, somewhat dulled and sad at heart, as one whose first gladness had received a chill. He could hear voices and see lights in other houses, whilst this one was so dark and still. Mrs. Clack had always warned him to keep himself to himself in the mews amongst her neighbours; and he obeyed her now as he had always done before. He did not go to inquire after her; but waited patiently at her door till something should happen.

At length he heard the crutches of cripple Jack coming limpingly along the court. Jack caught sight of him in the dusk, and stopped, leaning against the wall, as if ready to hold conversation with Don.

"She's gone," he said, nodding towards the empty house. "Dead!" cried Don, in a tone of profound terror. It struck Jack's mind that it would be worth while to see how far Don could be made a gull of, and he answered, without a moment's hesitation.

"Ay, dead!" he repeated, "and buried a week last Tuesday. She were raving and wandering just like the old man was before her. You could hear her across the mews, and she were calling for you over and over again, like this, 'Don! Don!'" and Jack imitated Mrs. Clack, as if she had been in the habit of shouting in a very loud voice.

"Dead!" uttered Don, thunderstruck with grief and dread.

"And buried the very next morning," continued Jack, enjoying his own success, and poor Don's sorrow; "the fever was so very strong on her, and the doctor had all the stores burned up, and the house locked, and the keys kept by the parish, so as nobody is to go into it for nobody knows how long. Some folks say the fever's got into the walls, and it's to be pulled down to the ground, but I don't know as that's true."

"And where's little Dot?" asked Don, after a short silence, rousing himself from his stupor a little.

"She's stopping a bit with the Watsons," he answered; "but you should only see Peggy thrashing her! It's only for a while though, for she's to be sent to the workhouse. I'm sorry for that, Don, I'm really sorry. She's a nice little thing, and very good; hardly ever whimpers so as you can hear her, no! not when Peggy whacks the hardest, and my! she can whack."

"She shan't ever go to the workhouse," said Don, in a low voice of resolution.

"Oh! I remember," went on Jack, chuckling to himself over Don's credulity, "the officer is coming to take her to-morrow morning at nine o'clock. There was nothing left from Mrs. Clack, after her funeral was paid for, and all the stores burnt up. So that made an end of everything, except Dot. Is there nothing more you'd like to ask me?"

"Nothing," answered Don, in the sickness of despair; "I wish you'd go away and leave me."

"Oh! I'll go," said Jack; "it's none so pleasant standing here, when you may catch the fever from the walls. So good-bye to you."

Don could not speak. The sudden calamity that had befallen him was too dreadful for words or tears. He had lost everything at one blow; and he felt bewildered and amazed at the sudden ruin of all his plans; his home was gone and his only friend. It did not occur to him to move away from the door-sill his feet had crossed so often, because it was infected and under a ban. Where was he to go to? where else could his weary limbs and heavy heart find a resting-place? He heard Jack's crutches clicking over the pavement, and then he was alone. Now Mrs. Clack was dead, he was utterly alone in the world.

By-and-by his ear caught the sound of a child crying in the dark, somewhere near at hand—of little Dot crying, for no other child in the mews cried softly and quietly like she did. He lifted himself up, and shook off the bewilderment of his sorrow; a new plan was already coming into shape in the lad's active brain. They should never carry off Dot to the dreadful workhouse, to be brought up with workhouse children. He thought of Peggy thrashing her, and his blood boiled. But he must keep himself quite still, and on the alert, unseen by anybody, if he was to carry out his scheme. He crouched down again in the darkness, and waited to and out where Dot was. Before long he discovered that she must be sitting at the foot of the narrow staircase leading up to the Watsons' rooms, and he crept silently that way, and as silently unlatched the door.

"Dot!" he breathed, in a very quiet tone; "hush, here's old Don."

"Don!" whispered the little creature, half afraid of him in the darkness.

"Ay! come along with old Don," he said, "and buy some sweeties. I've money in my pocket."

He put his arm gently round her, and she let him lift her up, and carry her away without a sound. Dot was accustomed to quiet movements and low voices, for her blind grandfather could not patiently endure any noise that could be spared him. And Don's manner towards her was very tender; he kissed the soft cheek next to him again and again, and he clasped her fondly in his arms. His heart sank as he passed Mrs. Clack's closed door, but he knew he had no time to linger. Cautiously he crept along the darkest side of the mews, where no lamp had been lit because of the broken glass; and he kept as much as possible in the dark along the streets, until he reached a distant place, where he could look at Dot in safety.

He sat down on the kerbstone in front of a brilliantly illuminated spirit vaults, where the glare of light fell full upon Dot's pretty face. It was dirty and unwashed, and her curly hair was in knots and tangles, through which he could hardly pass his fingers. The tears had made little channels down her cheeks; and the red cloak she had been so proud of was bespattered with mud. But she was laughing merrily now as she looked into his sorrowful face; and her little arms fastened round his neck again.

"Old Don!" she said, "old Don!"

"Ay! it's Don, little Dot," he answered, "and you belong all to me now. I'll take care of you, never fear. They say Jesus Christ is fond of little children, and He'd never like them to be beaten, or sent to the workhouse, I'm sure. You shan't go, though Mrs. Clack is dead."

His voice faltered as he uttered these last words, and the tears glistened in his eyes as Dot patted his cheek with her small hand.

"She's tomin' back aden," lisped Dot.

"No! never!" cried Don, breaking down into a passion of weeping, and hiding his face on Dot's curly head, "nobody ever comes back from where she's gone to," he sobbed. "But oh! she knew about God and Jesus Christ, and she wouldn't be so frightened to go, Dot. When I know all about God, I'll teach you and everybody else; so as nobody 'ul be afeared to die."

"She's tomin' back aden to-morrow," persisted Dot "She kissed me, and said good-bye, and went away, a long, long way off, where dere's flowers, and everything; but she said she'd tome back aden and take me some day. It's a bootiful place, old Don, and folks is kind to her dere. You shall tome too, old Don."

"Ay, ay! we'll go," he said, with a heavy sigh; "but, oh! it may be a long while first: and I've lots to learn before I'm fit to go to such a beautiful place. I know scarcely nothing yet, and I must set about learning all I can, though Mrs. Clack is dead."

It was time to seek a refuge for the night, but there was no difficulty about that, as Don had half a crown in his pocket, which had been given to him by some of his short-lived acquaintances at the sea-side. Don was only one among many who spent a few days at the Home, and then were lost again in the great multitudes that thronged London streets. With this half-crown, prudently laid out, he could provide food and lodging for himself and Dot, at least for the next two days and nights; and on Monday morning he must set to work somewhere, at something. He bought some little pies for their supper; and in the quietest corner of a crowded lodging-house, he fell fast asleep, worn out with grief and fatigue, and with little Dot safely protected by his arm. And as Don slept, he had a dream, a bright and vivid dream. It seemed, to him as if he had a brother, older than himself, and so wise, that all Mrs. Clack's wisdom was nothing to his. He was living far away, in a beautiful land; but Don dreamed there came a letter from him, written in letters of gold. It was so short that he could remember every word. It was this:

"DEAR DON,—There's plenty of room for you here, where I'm living; and I'll come for you, as soon as Dot is safe. Don't be troubled. I'll take care of you both."

But Don could not see the name at the end of the letter.

Chapter XII

Coming Home

When Mrs. Clack and Abbott, standing under Mrs. Watson's window, heard Peggy say that little Dot was lost, they felt the shock and chill of disappointment more for Hagar than for themselves. Abbott did not know the child at all; and Mrs. Clack's mind was full of the poor mother's broken-heartedness, described to her by him. They asked Peggy again and again when and how the child came to he lost, till the girl grew quite angry with their questioning.

"I'm sure I was as kind as kind could be," she said. "I was always giving her toffy and peppermint, and it was too bad of her to stray away, and get herself lost. But there I you know as much as I know, and I can't tell you no more. Father flogged me last night, and he says he'll flog me every night of my life till she's found. And she didn't belong to nobody that they should make such a fuss."

Peggy slammed the window down in her anger, and then opened it, and flung out Mrs. Clack's key without uttering a word. Abbott caught it in time to save Mrs. Clack's head; but her hand shook so much she could not fit it into the lock.

"Let me do it for you," he said, putting her on one side.

It was a very miserable coming home after the week's pleasure in the country. When the gas was lighted they could see how thickly the dust had settled upon everything, so that she was compelled to wipe a chair before she could ask Abbott to sit down.

She had stowed away most of the drapery which usually hung about the room before she left home; and the bare walls and bed-posts looked comfortless and strange to her. Besides, the bad news about Dot, and the stormy interview with Peggy had quite upset her, coming after the tranquillity and peace of her holiday. She sank down on one of the dusty chairs in a fit of great trembling.

"I did hope as God would have taken care of Dot for me," she faltered. It seemed very hard.

The child had been brought to her without any wish of her own; and she had put herself out of all her customary ways to care for her and the old man. She had nursed him through his illness and death, and tended her neighbour at much cost and sacrifice to herself. And now that she had come home refreshed and rested in body, and with her mind aroused with the pleasant thought of restoring Dot to her mother, it was a hard blow to find the child lost.

God is taking care of her," said Abbott, briefly. His face wore an expression of great disappointment also. He scarcely knew hmself how deep an interest he felt in Hagar's troubles; but he had ii ever felt a warmer glow of pleasure than he had done a few minutes ago, in the positive assurance that he was about to carry Dot home to her mother, awl be able to break to her the news of her father's death, whilst she was upheld by the delight of having her little girl once again in her arms. Still, the child could not be lost altogether; there were too many children among the poor for any one to wish to kidnap another, except for its good clothes; and Dot's clothing would not be very good. It was a great gain to know where she had been so lately as last evening; and surely it would not now be difficult to trace her. It was something, too, to know that Hagar's father had died peacefully in his bed, tended kindly by a good old woman like Mrs. Clack. Poor Hagar! She would not lie awake again long hours of the night, wondering where his old grey head was sheltering. He had been cared for as long as he lived: and he had escaped the doom he dreaded, that of dying in the workhouse.

"God bless you!" he said, "for all you've done for them. I'm going now to strike whilst the iron's hot. The little lass can't be far away. I'll come in again on Monday; tomorrow I run down to Birkenhead, stay there Sunday, and come back on Monday. But I'll send Hagar to you; and there's my address, if you hear aught of the child. Good-bye, Mrs. Clack.

The place looked still more forlorn and desolate when Abbott was gone. She could hardly believe it had ever seemed so solitary in the old times, when she had lived quite alone. Now the poor old blind fiddler was dead, Dot lost, and Don away; oh, how dreary and lonesome it was! What pleasure would the fresh eggs and yellow butter be to her if there was nobody to share them? But surely Don would be coming home soon, very soon. She had not heard of him for a fortnight, when Peggy had gone to the Fever Hospital to inquire after him; but he was nearly well then; and he must soon be dismissed. At any rate she would go and see after him to-morrow.

Somewhat comforted by this resolution, Mrs. Clack roused herself, and set about restoring her room to its accustomed appearance. She unwrapped and shook out two or three of the smartest gowns to decorate the bed-posts, and put the best bonnets she had in stock upon the top of them, and she clothed the bare walls with the gayest mantles and shawls. Home was looking like home again, and by-and-by her nervous depression was over; and she was ready to answer the door when she heard a low, single knock, very like Don's. It was not Don, however, but Peggy Watson, with a cracked tea-pot in her hand.

"Please, Mrs. Clack," she said, in a penitent voice, "I've made you a cup of good tea, and I'm very sorry I was so impudent. Father's come home and flogged me, and I never said a word against it. I'm sure I was good to little Dot—I was, indeed—and I'll go and search all London over fur her, till I've not got a sole to my foot."

"Have you heard anything of Don, Peggy?" asked Mrs. Clack.

"Oh yes! I've gone to the hospital again, out of my own head," she answered, "me and Dot, only he'd gone away from there to another hospital with a very hard name, down by the sea, and they said he'd come back as strong as a horse."

"That's good news;" said Mrs. Clack, taking the teapot out of Peggy's hand, and going back to her room with a feeling of relief. The damp chips and coal which had been sputtering and smouldering in the grate, were beginning to burn up brightly, and by the time her little tea-table was set ready beside the fire, she felt very much cheered and in better spirits.

"Well, God is taking care of Don," she said to herself, "that's quite plain, sending him down to the sea to get strong and well. And me too He's sent into the country, and it stands to sense, He'll take care of little Dot; He's not likely to overlook her, when He's so fond of little children. May be Mr; Abbott's found her already. Eh! it's a rare thing to be a man."

But Abbott had not found Dot, though he was hurrying from one police-station to another, describing her and her clothing, as he had heard them described by Hagar and Mrs. Clack. His description was vague enough, and he could learn nothing about the lost child. At last as he drew near home he met with a policeman who was carrying on his arm a little creature that had fallen fast asleep with its head upon his shoulder. Abbott stopped him to look at the sleeping face, and drowsy little head.

"I've never seen the child I'm seeking after," he said, "and I'm fairly puzzled; I can't tell for certain if this is the one. Age three, dark eyes—I cannot see the eyes—light, curly hair and fair skin, red cloak, brown hat, and blue frock, button shoes—but this child has lost its shoes—name Hagar, but answers to the name of Dot. Dot!" he called, patting the little cheek, "Dot!" but the child only answered by a sleepy cry, and nestled its head down again on the policeman's shoulder.

"I'm just going off my beat," he said; "and if you'll step with me as far as the station, I'll come round with you to Hawthorne Road, and take the child with me. It's no more than a step out of my way."

It was past midnight when Abbott and the policeman turned into Hawthorne Road, and all the houses were dark and silent, except his own. He was five hours behind his time, and he knew very well that the two women standing on the door-steps, looking out anxiously, could be no other than his cousin and

Hagar. Was he really bringing home her child to her? He did not know what she would do if this was not Dot.

The steady tread of their footsteps sounded loudly in the silent street, and reached the ears of the anxious women long before they could see who was coming. Hagar was the first to catch sight of Abbott, and of the policeman carrying a little child in his arms; she could see the curly head resting on his shoulder, as he passed under the lamps. Her heart seemed to stand still, and her limbs felt heavy and rigid, as if they would not move at her will. But with a great effort she recovered herself, and darting down the road, she met them before they could reach the house. She snatched the 'child, her child, from the policeman, and sank down on the pavement, clasping it closely to her bosom.

"Hagar! Hagar!" exclaimed Abbott. "I'm not sure it's Dot. I never saw your little lost girl. Look at her face, and see. Only you can tell if it's Dot."

She hardly dared to lift up the drowsy face, or fix heir own eyes upon it. Her arms relaxed their hold, and again her heart seemed to cease its rapid throbbing. Abbott caught the little creature, and held it under her failing eyes, and then Hagar, with a low moan, pushed it away, and fell senseless to the ground.

Chapter XIII

Dot and Don in the World

It was hard work to Abbott to leave home the next morning before Hagar was awake from the miserable restless slumber into which she had fallen after recovering from her swoon. It was as hard work as when his mother lay dying. He must be away three days, but there was no help for it. "Men must work, and women must weep,"—and with a heavy heart, and spirits more down than his comrades had ever known him to be, he set out for his three days' absence.

One idea was firmly rooted in Don's mind—that the whole force of the police with all the parish offices, even to the parish doctor, were in a band, set upun catching little Dot, and confining her in the dismal prison of a workhouse. He had heard terrible stories of that unknown place; stories which had made his flesh creep and his soul rebel against the thought of ever entering it himself, or suffering any one else to meet so fearful a lot. Old Lister's strong hatred of it had increased his own dread. Could he consent to little Dot being shut up within those dreary walls, and having her merry little life crushed out of her? Don was ready to die first.

The first and chief thing to be done was to throw their pursuers off the scent; and Don took as many precautions as if all the millions of London folks were avowed enemies, seeking to snatch Dot from him. He made his way to the East End with cunning changes of his route; dodging from street to alley, and from alley to street; threading the thickest mazes of courts and passages where a policeman was seldom if ever seen. He made it impossible to trace his course. When Dot was tired he carried her till his arms ached; or he sat clown in the shelter of a doorway, nursing her carefully on his knees that no damp should strike to her from the stone steps. Every word she said, every smile on her little face, was precious to him. God, he thought, had given to him the charge of saving the child from a fearful doom; and he was bent upon fulfilling the charge to the utmost.

Late in the evening they found themselves in a poor alley not far from the docks; and as Don had still half of his money left, he again sought the shelter of a lodging-house, and gave the woman who kept it one of his few pennies to wash Dot's face and hands.

it was Sunday the next day; and he left the close lodging-house early, not with any idea of getting work, for he had been taught at the Convalescent Home that he must do no manner of work on a Sunday; and he was determined upon faithfully obeying God's laws, as far as he knew them. But he had only sevenpence left; and if he did nothing to earn a few pence all day, he must make a choice between hunger and houselessness when night came back again. He could not buy both food for the day, and shelter for the night. If he had been alone nothing would have prevented him from satisfying the cravings of his hunger; but there was little Dot to consider. There could be no question as to whether she could bear the cold of a March night spent out of doors. He bought a penny loaf, and begged a drop of milk for her, from a good natured-looking woman, who kept a little shop at a corner of a street, and who gave him a few stale crusts that were beginning to get mouldy. Don made a feast of them on the first empty doorstep they came to. He felt as if he could go without any more food that day, and if he could satisfy Dot they might still be able to pay for a shelter at night.

He had time, now that his most pressing cares were over, to think of Mrs. Clack at leisure. Dot was playing up and down the steps beside him in the court where they had breakfasted, and there was no immediate anxiety to divert his thoughts. How good Mrs. Clack had been to him! He remembered his dark sleeping-place, and the hard old mattress he had been used to lie upon, with a painful choking in his throat. And Mr's. Clack's fireside, where he had spent many a warm, peaceful evening, often never uttering a word, but watching wonderingly her serious face as she sat reading her book, or making up her accounts, and counting out her money. What a clever, knowing, wise woman she was; and always so good to him!

Could it be only two days since he bade good-bye to the folks at the Convalescent Home, and journeyed back to London with high hopes and gay spirits? At the time he had been at the seaside, he had been treasuring up in his memory strange things to tell her, and important questions to ask her. His teachers down there had told him very wonderful stories about God and Jesus Christ which he had loved to listen to; but he was hardly prepared to give them full faith till he had heard what Mrs. Clack had to say. It was so strange that she should never have told him such good news as the words he had learned by heart, "God so loved the world, that He gave His only begotten Son, that whosoever believeth in Him should not perish, but have everlasting life." Mrs. Clack knew about Jesus Christ; she had spoken His name to old Lister when he lay dying; and he should be sure she would not deceive him in any way. Very grand and beautiful the words quite sounded; but how was he to be sure they were true now Mrs. Clack was dead?

Don covered his face with his hands to hide the tears stealing down his cheeks. But this was a signal to Dot that he was inclined to play at bo-peep; and she clapped her little hands, and pulled at him, and laughed merrily, till he was forced to uncover his sad face, and begin to play with her. But his heart was heavy in spite of the game amid little Dot's merriment. Oh, how good Mrs. Clack had been to him; and now she was dead.

"What's the matter, youngster?" asked a policeman, who was sauntering past, and stopped to look at Don's sorrowful attempts at play.

"Nothink, sir!" he cried, starting to his feet in alarm, and catching Dot up in his arms.

"Your little sister, eh?" said the policeman, idly.

"She's my little gel," he answered in haste. "Nobody belongs to her or me. I'm all she's got, and she's all I've got."

"All right, my lad," he said, slowly pacing on, whilst Don looked after him, his heart beating, and his limbs trembling with the shock of fear. He was not as strong as a horse yet, in spite of his fortnight at the seaside. As soon as the dreaded policeman was out of sight, he crept away to another and poorer street, and sat down in a more out-of-the-way corner. The church bells were ringing and chiming from one tower after another; and fell pleasantly on his ear.

"It's Sunday, God's own day," he said to little Dot; "and we mustn't work on Sundays. I hardly know why; but if God wishes it I won't, and p'raps He'll give me good luck to-morrow. They told me I ought to go to church on Sunday; those great, big churches that are kep' locked up all week. They're God's own houses, they said; and we ought to go there on God's days, when they are open. I don't think the folks 'ud like you and me to go—we're not fine enough, Dot, and may be they'd be asking us questions. So we'll stay here and keep quiet and snug; and God won't miss us amongst such a many."

"I want to go," said Dot, pouting for a moment.

"Ay! we'll go some day," he answered, "when I've picked up lots o' money, and bought you a pretty frock. I'd like my little gel to go to God's house, but I must work hard, and learn hard; and Dot shall be one of God's little children, as can read and write and sing. There was a little gel once Jesus Christ called back again after she was dead. Oh! I wish He'd been by to call Mrs. Clack back again!"

"She's tomin' back aden," asserted Dot, positively; and as Don took no notice of her, being plunged once more into the depths of grief, she danced up and down before him, singing, "She's tomin' back aden, old Don; she's tomin' back aden."

By dint of fasting all day, and persuading Dot to eat stale bread which he bought cheaply, and soaked in the water at a drinking-fountain, Don had fourpence remaining when night fell. He knew well enough that the charge would be sixpence for himself and Dot, fourpence if he had been alone. With an anxious heart he made his way back to his lodging of time night before, and laid down his four pennies on the landlady's table by the door. He was passing on, holding Dot fast by the hand, when the woman stopped him.

"There's the little girl," she said.

"I haven't got a penny left, not one farthing," answered Don, with desperate earnestness, "and it's a bitter cold night, or we'd have slept out of doors. I'd leave her alone, and sleep out myself, but she'd be cryin' all night, and what could you do with her? We'll only take up as much room as one; and I'll pay you as soon as ever I can."

The woman looked out into the dark street, and saw the March rain and sleet drifting before the wind. Little Dot was half asleep already, clinging drowsily to Don's hand. The landlady nodded silently, and beckoned him to go on into the close warm room beyond. When Don stretched his weary limbs upon the miserable bed, gnawed with hunger as he was, but with little Dot safe and sleeping peacefully beside him, a smile came across his face, and he whispered, as if he hoped some ear would hear him, "Thank you, God!"

"Never mind about that twopence," said the land-lady to him, the next morning, "I'd a little girl myself once, like your little sister there. You'd not like to give her up to me, I s'pose? I'd be very good to her."

"No, no!" cried Don, in terror, drawing Dot closer to him. If the woman grew tired of her, or cross with her, she might send her to the workhouse, or turn her into the streets. No, he could not give her up; he could never forsake her. Oh! if only his dream had been true, and he had a brother taking care of him, as he took care of little Dot!

Chapter XIV

No Sign from God

The shock to Hagar of thinking her child was found, and then discovering it to be a mistake, threw her back once more in health both of body and mind. She did not mourn greatly when they told her of her father's death; it was almost a relief to learn that he had died quietly, and that his sufferings and wanderings were ended. But the mysterious disappearance of Dot, and the utter failure of all Abbott's efforts to trace her preyed upon her depressed spirits. Mrs. Clack's companionship seemed to comfort her more than any other; and when work was slack at the dressmaker's she would go to stay with her for a day or two, in the little room that had been Dot's last home, repaying the old woman by the skill with which she re-made the cast-off wardrobes she had purchased, and which she sold again more profitably after Hagar's clever fingers had been at work upon them.

Mrs. Clack had her own personal and special grief in the non-appearance of Don, whose return she had hopefully anticipated. If any one could find Dot again, it would be Don. She went to inquire after him at the fever hospital, and was referred to the Convalescent Home, but her letter to the matron there brought back the news that he had had his fare paid up to London, and had been actually seen into the train, but nothing had been heard of him since, though he had promised faithfully to get Mrs. Clack to write for him. They were disappointed in Don, who had seemed a very promising and grateful boy. As week after week passed by, and no Don appeared, Mrs. Clack was compelled to give him up, and mourn over him as lost to her for a time. No one had seen him, except the cripple, and he had grown too much afraid of the consequences to confess the cruel trick he had played upon him.

The summer was bright and warm, with a long continuance of pleasant weather. The hardships of London life abated, and the poorest and feeblest found a brief season of release from crushing poverty. The children passed the livelong summer days out of doors, some of the boldest pushing their way out of the sultry streets to the green freshness of the parks. The trees in Kensington Gardens were full of leaf, and the high branches meeting and arching over head, formed a thick and welcome shade from the hot sun. The thrushes and blackbirds sang as blithely, and the rooks cawed amidst their nests in the topmost forks of the tall elms, as if there were no noise and smoke of a busy city all about them. Once or twice in the cool of the evening Abbott heard the soft low cooing of a wood pigeon where the trees were thickest, uttered shyly amidst the bold and constant twittering of hundreds of other birds in the leafy branches above him. He tried to persuade Hagar to enter the Gardens, but in vain; she could not conquer her sorrowful dread of them. She shut herself up day after day of the summer time, in her hot little attic under the roof.

"Hagar," he said one evening, when he went up to see her, and found her with a worn face and thin fingers, stitching away at some work without pause or rest. "Hagar, you want a sign that God loves you and forgives you. Would it help you if I told you I love you, though I know all you've done? If you'd only be my wife I'd do all I could to make you happy again."

"It's out of pity," answered Hagar, dropping her work, and lifting up her bowed head to look at him.

"Ay I it was pity at first," he said, "I know it was pity, but it's love now. I'm thinking of you day and night, and pondering over what I can do for you; how I can comfort you. I can't find little Dot; but if you'll be my wife, I'll love you truly, and do all I can to make you happy."

"I don't deserve to be happy," replied Hagar, weeping. "If I'd only known God then as I know Him now, I couldn't have forsook them; and suppose we'd died together somewhere, it would be better than being as I am now. I can't forgive myself; and I can't see how God can forgive me. He can't undo the wicked thing I did; and there's no misery like being wicked. But I'll try to believe God loves me. Some day or other, perhaps, He'll let me know I am forgiven; even if I never find little Dot,"

"And some day," said Abbott, "you'll be my wife."

"I couldn't be," she answered, looking at him steadfastly, with her dark, sunken eyes; "I'm too heavy laden with trouble yet. I couldn't be happy in heaven itself. I know God must let us feel how bitter sin is, or we might fall into it again. It's right I should be sorrowful for what I've done. I should only make you miserable too if I was your wife now."

"Must I find Dot before you will marry me?" he asked, patiently, seeing how deep her trouble was.

"Oh!" she cried, "if she is not found soon, I shall not know her again; little children change so! it's eight months already since I saw her; and if she's been ill, or if any accident's happened to her, she might be changed past knowing again. That's what I'm afraid of always. Suppose she was a year or two in the workhouse, and grew like the workhouse children, perhaps I might see her and not know her again. I might feel as if it was her, and never be quite sure!"

"I'll try again, Hagar," said Abbott, "and if we don't find her before then, we'll be married next Easter at the farthest. That's seven months to come, and you'll be more at peace in yourself; or if not, we'll bear the burden of your trouble together. If I cannot make you happy, you will not make me miserable, I know."

There was a faint smile in Hagar's eyes, though she shook her head dejectedly.

"You are too good. for me," she answered, "you're the best friend I ever had; but perhaps some day you'll be worn out too, and forsake me. It would only he what I deserve, and I shan't blame you."

Yet in spite of herself it roused and gladdened Hagar's heart to believe that Abbott, who knew all about her, loved her well enough to wish to make her his wife. His search after Dot, which had slackened a little, was renewed with more persevering energy than before; and Hagar, as she grew less downcast, entered into it more earnestly. Yet it was almost a hopeless pursuit, and grew more and more hopeless as the autumn succeeded summer, and itself faded into the chilly dreariness of winter. They followed up the faintest track, and caught up the vaguest rumours of lost children; but with no success. Many a child had been found straying about the streets since March, and had been carried to the workhouse; but not one of them was Dot.

"It's a year next Sunday since I forsook them," said Hagar one day, as they were returning, baffled and dispirited, from some fruitless search, "and if you like, I'll go into the Gardens then."

It was just such another day as the dreary day last November. The yellow fog hung about the trees; and drops of rain fell from the bare branches upon the muddy sward below. There were very few people about though it was Sunday afternoon; and Abbott and Hagar walked along the sodden paths, undisturbed by the sound of voices or the foot-fall of passers-by.

"If I'd only kept true!" said Hagar, lifting her pale face to the gloomy sky, "if I'd only thought of God, and kept true to them! God does love us; I believe it now: but oh! if I'd only known it then, and waited, and seen what He would have done for us. There's the very tree I left my father under; he stood just there, listening as I went away; and little Dot was playing off yonder among the trees, hiding behind them for me to go and find her! How could I be so cruel? It's right I shouldn't find her now. Oh! what a wicked, wicked thing it was to do!"

"But you have repented sorely," said Abbott.

"Yes, sorely, sorely," sobbed Hagar, "God forgives; you say so, and I believe it. I don't think He's angry with me now, and I'm going to try to be a real Christian. But oh! to think of little Dot, playing there among the trees, and never to see her again, and never to know what has become of her! I feel as if I didn't know how much I loved her. I couldn't ever forsake her now. It isn't baby I grieve for, for he's safe and happy in heaven, and my poor father, he's quiet in the grave. But, Dot! I'd be glad to find her lying dead yonder among the trees where I left her playing, rather than never know what's happened to her."

"Cannot you trust her to God?" he asked, gently. "You forget what the Lord Jesus said whilst He was yet alive, when He called a little child unto Him, 'It is not the will of your Father which is in heaven that one of these little ones should perish.' You do not yet believe that God loves your child more than you love her yourself; ay, and can take care of her better. He can never forget or forsake her."

"Oh! I'll try to believe it," she answered, with deep-drawn sobs; "I do try to believe all you tell me about God! But, oh! if I'd kept true to them then!"

She said no more, but paced mournfully along the paths she had trodden when she wandered about the Gardens in the night, with her baby slumbering at times, and wailing at times on her bosom. She recalled it all, and fixed it afresh upon her memory, as if she feared it might fade away. Abbott walked beside her in silence, in pitiful patience, until they left the gardens by the gate where she had fallen under the horse's feet in the darkness of the November morning, and he had first seen her in her utter misery and poverty.

"I'll try to be a good wife to you," she said, as they stood still for a few moments, thinking each of them of that morning "You are very good to me, and I shall get over it in time may be; but if I'm ever down hearted and very sorrowful, you'll know what I'm thinking oft, and you'll bear with me?"

"Ay! God helping me," he answered heartily, "you shall be a happy woman yet, Hagar."

Chapter XV

Don's Thanksgiving

Don began his new task with great energy—the task of providing for little Dot's wants. Fortunately for him the worst part of the winter was over; though the nights were still cold, and many of the spring days were too stormy for a young child to live altogether out of doors. But the daylight lasted long, and the times were busy; it was just the season of the year when work was most plentiful. Even at the East End there was a difference when the West End was filled with its population of wealthy people. From the earliest dawn till the latest twilight Don was sharply on the look-out for any job to be done, and his keen eyes and quick movements often secured him work wherever there was a press of business on hand.

Sometimes Dot trotted beside him, or rode on his shoulders, when he went on errands. His happiest days were those when he had a little money to lay out in oranges, or vegetables, or other small marketable stock, which promised him a quick return, and a good profit on his outlay. Then Dot rode triumphantly on his hired wheel-barrow, keeping him merry with her little ways, and the chatter he loved to listen to. But he often found that she could not go with him when he was bound for any distance, or was engaged for a few hours' work, and then, with sore misgivings of heart, and countless terrors, while he was away, he was compelled to leave her in the charge of some lodging-house keeper, or, still oftener, under the chance care of some apple-stall woman, near his place of work, whose stall might happen to be in an archway, or any other sheltered spot: The women were very good to little Dot, but it caused him many a pang of anxiety, and many a sharp sense of gladness, first to leave her, and then to come back and find her safe and happy.

The wandering life they led was very pleasant to him, and Dot throve well upon it. They scarcely ever spent a week in the same lodging-house, or even in the same street; though Don kept cautiously to the East End, and the neighbourhood of the Docks, where he could almost always find some work to do. In his eagerness to be earning money for Dot and her wants, he pitted himself against full-grown men, and thrust himself forward for tasks too heavy for him. He could not get rid of his dread of the child being forcibly taken away from him, if there was anything miserable and neglected about her appearance. To ask any person for help or advice in any way would subject him to questions he could not easily and truthfully answer. If he found any of the people with whom she was thrown into company at all desirous to know his history, it was a sufficient hint to him to change his quarters; and any kindly inquiry from the women who took care of Dot for him, filled him with deep anxiety. Amid all his ignorance he knew he must not tell a lie; and he could not bring himself to break the law of the God of whom he had so faint a knowledge, even when facing the danger of losing little Dot. If he could only say she was his sister, that would be a sufficient answer to every inquiry, but Don could not. To speak the truth always, and to teach Dot to do the same, was what God required of him, and he must do it.

As a further precaution against being tracked and discovered by Dot's enemies, the police and parish authorities of Chelsea, who were bent upon imprisoning her in the workhouse, he dropped the name of Don, which he knew by this time to be too odd and singular to escape notice, and called himself John. He tried hard to call Dot "Haggar," which he believed was her real name, as old Lister had once said she was christened after the mother who had forsaken her. But he seldom succeeded in remembering her new name, except when anybody asked him what to call her. Still, having taken these cautious measures, he felt he had raised yet another barrier against the chance of her detection by her West End foes.

The summer was very welcome to Don, and the long, light warm evenings were full of pleasure to him. Then, after the day's hard work was done, he could carry Dot down to the side of the river, and watch the ships passing up and down, with their gaily-coloured flags floating idly on the soft western wind, and he would wonder with the quiet wondering of ignorance where they were going to and where they came from.

He had seen them sailing with all their canvas spread on the open sea, looking even more beautiful and strange than on the river, and the sight of them brought back those pleasant days when he was growing slowly better from the fever, and was treasuring up stories to talk over with Mrs. Clack. The ships, with their tall masts and the white sails, recalled to him some of the lessons he had learned about God, and Jesus Christ, and Heaven—names which were little more than mere words to him, yet which had a power over him no other words possessed. They were like good seed buried deep in the good ground of his faithful heart, promising to bring forth a hundredfold at some future harvest-tide.

Don was growing very tall during these lightsome summer days; but he grew thinner and weaker as if he was outgrowing his strength. He was always hungry, and hunger is a costly comrade to poor folks. It had to be tricked, and put off, and mastered, instead of being satisfied. What gave him more real concern was that he had quite outgrown his clothes, and was no longer decent-looking enough to be entrusted with errands. He grudged buying anything for himself which Dot could not share, or as long as there was any want of hers not supplied. Dot did not look as if she suffered any want; and he loved to see her pretty face look rosy and smiling. She never cried softly now, as if afraid of being heard; it was seldom that she cried at all, but if she did it was quite openly, and noisily enough to frighten Don. He would not let her suffer from hunger and cold, and the fresh air from the river made her strong and active, and gave her a ravenous appetite, which Don satisfied, whilst he put off his own sharp-set cravings. It was quite necessary to live on short commons, if he had to provide himself with larger clothes.

It was a proud day to him when he had saved enough to buy a new jacket and trousers second-hand in Rag Fair. He had had his eye upon them for some days past, and every time his work took him that way, he had run through the market to see if they were still hanging up for sale. They had even had the price reduced by sixpence, which enabled him to buy them a day sooner. He drove a hard bargain for them, giving his old ones as part of the price, and changing them before he left the place. The salesman told him it was a man's suit, and that he stood up like a man in it; though Don's tall thin frame, and his long pale face looked very little like a man in his strength.

"Little Dot," he said, fondly, as he took the child's small hand into his own, and led her away from the noisy market, "tomorrow's Sunday, and now I've got some new clothes, you and me'll go into one of the big churches, into the very biggest of 'em, Dot, where we've never been before. God is sure to be in the biggest of 'em, and I'm going to thank Him for my new clothes, and everythink. We can't never see Him, you know, but He'll be there, and you and me'll both say, Thank you, won't we, Dot?"

"I'll say sank 'ou, old Don," answered Dot, "and p'raps He'll give me some new clothes, and buns, and pies, and a pritty lady doll."

"It's God as gives us everythink," said Don.

Very early next day they were up and away out of the close atmosphere of the lodging-house, into the sweet fresh air of the summer morning. Don washed Dot's face in a horse-trough under a drinking-fountain, and gave himself an unusually careful toilet, being very eager to present a creditable appearance at the door of St. Paul's Cathedral. They were there an hour or two before the time for the morning service, and Don looked up, with a new sense of interest and awe at the massive pile of building he was going to enter for the first time. As if he had never seen them until now, he gazed upwards at the great statues, standing clearly out against the deep blue of the sky, and wondered who they were, and why they should be placed up yonder. The golden cross above the dome, raised highest of all, glittered brightly in the sunshine; but he did not know the meaning of it. It did not speak to Don of the Lord Jesus Christ, the Brother and the Saviour of man.

Nevertheless Don's soul was full of gentle and grateful feelings towards God. There was very much for him to give thanks for; He had saved Dot from her enemies, and from hunger and cold: Dot had never been very hungry, and had never slept out of doors on a bad night. And if he had suffered from cold and hunger himself, it was not worth thinking of—thousands of boys shared the same fate, and he must not grumble. He did not doubt that the good luck he had met with came from God, and now He had given to him a man's suit, which he could never grow out of There was quite a tremor of gladness and thankfulness in his heart, which could only be calmed by giving thanks to God in His own house.

At last, wearied out with standing, he sat down close beside the door of the cathedral, with Dot on his lap, and waited patiently, until a little knot of people began to gather round the entrance. As the great bell struck the time for opening, they could hear footsteps within the walls, and Don, with a beating heart, rose to his feet, and seized Dot -tightly by the hand. He listened to the key turning in the lock, and time creaking of the hinges, as the door opened, and then of all the multitude that entered St. Paul's that summer Sunday, Dot and Don were the first to cross the threshold.

But what a vast and solemn place it seemed to Don! After his first few eager paces into the cathedral, he stood awestruck and trembling, gazing upwards at the high roof overhead, and onward to the shining window in the east, which seemed very far from him. A verger passing by bade him sharply to take his cap off, and he not only hastened to obey him, but he removed Dot's old brown hat as well, and they stood bare-headed in this house of God. He felt frightened yet glad. It was some time before he ventured to take a seat; at the very end of a long row of chairs, upon which he sank down, with a deep sigh of bewilderment almost amounting to terror. He felt himself altogether in another world from the world outside. There was nothing here like his common life.

The deep-toned organ, and the sweet singing of the choir bewildered him still more. He had never heard anything like it, and he could not understand a single word. He knelt down when those about him knelt, and stood up when they stood—why, he did not know. When the chanting ceased, he could hear afar off a single voice, but what that voice was saying he could not tell.

It was all wonderful, all splendid, all vague to him. It seemed to throw him a long way off from God; for how could he ever learn to pray like this? For a little while his spirits sank very low within him as he listened and wondered, watching the white robed boys who seemed so much at home in that solemn place. Could he ever become like one of them? Who would teach him what he ought to do?

Yet when the service was ended, and the congregation were loitering inquisitively about the monuments which surrounded them on every hand, Don lifted up his eyes to the angels in the shining window in the east; and with a feeling that God must be very present in this strange and awful place, he whispered in a low, almost inaudible voice, "Thank you, God, for everythink."

He turned away with a relieved heart, as if the dim dread of never knowing how to serve God had fallen from him. God was very good to him, though he did not know how to pray like the boys he had been wondering at. It was only noon-day when he and Dot left the cathedral but for all the remaining hours of that pleasant summer Sunday, as they lingered about the bridges, and by the river-side, Don was happy, happier than he had ever been in his life before.

Chapter XVI

Not Long for this World

But summer cannot last for ever. The autumn came early, with a long season of rainy days and gloomy skies, unbroken by sunshine. Don did not know it, but the gathering in of the harvest had been a bad one; for frequent and heavy thunder-storms had damaged the crops, and the country had lost millions of money by the failure of its corn-fields. It brought in a hard winter for the poor, and higher prices for the food they had to buy. The rise in flour and bread was not enough to cause anxiety in households moderately well-off, or where work was certain; but to Don, and to thousands like him living from hand to mouth, a smaller penny loaf was a serious calamity. The bakers, too, were more careful of their stale bread, and not so ready to give it away for nothing; even when little Dot's bonny face was lifted up eagerly to them across the counter.

Yet Don did not lose heart, or for a moment entertain a passing thought of giving up Dot to the fate he dreaded for her. He never knew now what it was to have the gnawing sense of hunger quite pacified; but he was a boy, almost a man, he said to himself proudly, and he could bear to be starved and pinched, though a tender little child-like Dot could not. She hampered him, and hindered him from undertaking work by which he could have earned much more money than by doing any chance task that fell in his way. The constant watchfulness which his dread for her forced upon him, made it necessary that she should be always somewhere at hand, that he might assure himself of her safety. If he was hanging about the docks seeking for work, Dot was sure to be close by, sitting by the charcoal fire of some chestnut-roaster or under the shelter of a fruit-stall. The fear of having her snatched away from him began to haunt him more, and to fill him with sharper care. He could hardly bear to lose sight of her; but it hindered him from getting on.

The gloomy autumn crept insensibly into the winter mouths, when the days were shortest, and the hours of work, with the chances of earning money, were few. Don had less to do, and more time to rest, but he was always weary, and every doorstep seemed to tempt him to sit down and take breath awhile. It was so long since be had rested himself in a chair, that he could hardly remember how easy and comfortable were the chairs in that hospital by the sea-side, where his last taste of home-comfort had been. To sit on doorsteps and the stone benches of the bridges, or on bits of planks and spare bricks, was all the rest he had had for many a month. He had not given a thought to it before; but when all his limbs ached, and his very bones felt weary as they always did now, the remembrance came back to him vividly of the cushioned rocking-chair by Mrs. Clack's warm fire, where he had been allowed to sit sometimes, nursing little Dot upon his knee. Dot often sat upon his knee still; but how soon he tired of her light weight! Still Don had a good fund of hope and courage within him, which kept him from sinking beneath his weariness and hunger. A few more months to struggle through, and summer would be here once more, and all those sunny evenings by the river-side would come again. He had some plans for learning to read during the winter; and he had already put them so far into practice as to prevail upon two or three persons who knew how to read, to teach him a few verses in the little book of texts which had been given to him at the Convalescent Home. Fortunately some of the verses had been marked out by having a black line drawn round them; and the matron had told him those were the texts she most wished him to learn. His first verse was, "The Son of Man is come to seek and to save that which is lost' The words were so simple that he could learn them easily. But who was the Son of Man?

Those persons whom he ventured to ask were as ignorant as himself, or if they, knew, they either laughed at him or bade him hold his tongue. They did not care to think of Him in the midst of the dreary, miserable, vicious lives they were living. Yet the words had a pleasant melody in them to Don, something like the wonderful music he had heard in St. Paul's Cathedral; and often he repeated them to himself and little Dot: "The Son of Man is come to seek and to save that which is lost."

All through the chilly autumn, and the dark winter, the little child was thriving, and living happily, even among the squalid hardships of the circumstances surrounding her. Whatever Don went without, Dot had enough, as long as he could procure it for her, and, like all little children, having food and clothing she was quite content. A home Don could not provide for her; and now and then, though the weather was not very wintry yet, she suffered something from the rain and cold. Still his love and care for her preserved her from much harm; her face continued rosy and plump; and she was growing fast, so fast that Don willingly believed it was her increasing size and weight which made her so heavy a burden to him, that now he could no longer carry her even a few yards. Dot was a chattering, playful, merry little creature so full of fun that Don would often carry on a game with her when the perspiration stood thick -upon his forehead, and his breath came fitfully and painfully through his pale lips.

It came to pass at last that it seemed as if he could not get any work to do. When an errand-boy was wanted, busy people shook their heads at him, and chose somebody else. If a small burden was entrusted to him, eager as he was to carry it, he would stagger under the weight along the pavements, and be scarcely able to make his way through the throng of passers-by. To earn money was becoming so difficult as to be almost impossible.

One day, as he went to fetch Dot away, after having left her in charge of a friendly apple-woman, who had her stall against the Tower railings, he overheard her say to another woman near her, as he moved languidly away, "Poor lad! he isn't long for this world!" Don turned back, with his sunken face, and wasted, weary limbs.

"Is it me, missis?" he asked.

"What?" said the woman.

"Me as isn't long for this world?" he repeated.

"Oh, dear me!" she answered, cheerily, "that doesn't mean much to be feared of."

"I don't know whatever 'ud become of little Dot," he said, wistfully.

But though he tried to believe it could not be himself they were speaking of, he was not deceived. He dragged his feeble steps along, with Dot dancing and jumping beside him, till they reached a quieter spot in one of the narrow streets near at hand; and then he sat down to think. He did not feel as if anything ailed him, except that he was very weary, and he longed to lie down and sleep once again on his old mattress in Mrs. Clack's store-room. He was never hungry now, he could go without food longer, much longer than he could two months ago, and feel no gnawing or craving for it. The very smell of bread in the bakers' shops seemed to satisfy him. Yet he could not altogether he sure that the women were wrong. He could feel all the bones in his wasted limbs; and his clothes, the man's suit he was so proud of, hung upon him as if he was a skeleton. People died of starvation sometimes in London; but surely this ailment of his, if he was ailing, could not be starvation, it had come on so slowly. But suppose it should be true that he was not long for this world!

Don buried his face in his hands, to shut out all other impressions, except the painful thought that possessed him. If he should die, what would become of little Dot? There would be no home for her, no friend, no lot but that of the dreaded workhouse, from which he had striven so hard to save her. That was a very bitter thought. And if he died he should die because he had tried to save her. That was still more bitter. To die, failing to do what you have given your life for—could any sorrow be like that sorrow? Don was overwhelmed; himself dead, and little Dot a workhouse girl—that was what lay before them.

Then into his troubled heart there came a deep, resistless longing to visit once more the haunts of bygone days where he had been strong and happy. He knew no more why he wished to see again the place where his friend Mrs. Clack had given him a home, than the swallow knows why it seeks again the eaves where it built its nest last year. For a little while, as he sat there motionless, seeing and hearing nothing, he lived over again the old ti rues, until he almost forgot his weariness and weakness. But Dot roused him before long from his reverie. It was too late to start on such a journey' to-night; for it would take a long while to cross London at his pace, and he must give himself time for many a rest by the way. But tomorrow he would go to Chelsea, and just look round at the old places once more; lest it should be too late, if it was true that he was not long for this world.

It was past the middle of January, and already the days were lengthening out a little, both at sunrise and sunset; but Don started off with Dot, whom he dared not leave behind him, before the chilly, wintry dawn came. Even Dot had to set out without breakfast, for their last halfpenny was spent, and no shop was open where they dared go in, and beg for a morsel of bread. Now and then Don's head grew giddy, and his feet staggered under him; and he was compelled to take long rests, wherever he could find a resting-place in the busy thoroughfares they were passing through. He lay along one of the benches in the park for an hour or more, while Dot played about him, and strange and pleasant dreams thronged through his brain, dreams which brought a smile to his face, and laughter to his pale lips. He could not have put them into words, for Don knew very few words. But these dreams filled his head with feelings as wonderful and beautiful as the sounds he had heard and the sights he had seen when he went up to St. Paul's to render his thanks-giving unto God.

At length the long and painful pilgrimage was over; and they had but to wait an hour or two for the twilight to fall, before they could enter the mews where Mrs. Clack had been used to live. For Don was still full of fears, and of vague hopes for Dot; and he was not willing to give her up to her enemies while there was any chance for her. It might not be true that he was going to be taken from her, and his strength might come again. He would not give up all for lost yet. He was merely going to creep into the old court, arid have a last long look at the place, the only place in the world that had ever been anything like a home to him. Then he and Dot would face the cold and cruel world once more, until he conquered, or was altogether crushed in the battle.

Under the shadows of the dusk, which gathered early in the narrow mews, with tall houses all about it, Don crawled along the worn pavement to the well-known door, and sank down exhausted on the doorsill, hushing Dot, lest her voice should betray them. Oh! how often he had crossed this sill with a light heart! If Mrs. Clack could but come back from the grave where they had buried her, and be waiting for him and Dot, as she had so often done in those old times! He could hear a quiet footstep moving about in the room upstairs, as he had often heard hers; amid by-and-by the gas was lit, and its little gleam of light shone out across the court, and into the darkness which hid them. Just as it had been in old times! He was right glad he had come, though the way had been toilsome, and he was worn out and weary. He would put Dot out of sight in an out-of-tire-way corner he knew of; and then he would knock at the door, and ask who lived there now, if it was only to look up the old staircase again.

"Little Dot shall hide herself," ho said, "and old Don'll find her again in a minute."

He left the child, and with a throbbing heart and a trembling hand he rapped at the door, holding his breath to listen. There was a quiet step coining deliberately clown the stairs, just like Mrs. Clack's; and the door opened, and there stood Mrs. Clack herself!

Chapter XVII

Homewards

Don stood speechless before Mrs. Clack, whilst his large, glistening eyes were fastened on her face, and his lips moved Without uttering a word, as if she had been indeed one risen from the dead. He could hardly believe that he saw aright, and he dared not stretch out his hand, even if he had possessed the strength, to touch her and make sure she was no vision.

Mrs. Clack's first feeling was one of great gladness, for she had mourned over Don, as one who had strayed away for a little while, possibly into bad ways, but who would come home at last, like the prodigal son driven by famine to his father's house. Here was Don back again, and she was full of joy, until, looking more closely into his pinched and shrunken face, with the temples falling into hollows, and the glassy eyes shining hungrily, as if he was starved to the very point of dying, a sudden shock of distress and terror ran through her.

"Why, Don!" she cried, catching both of his wasted hands in her own, "Don, my boy! where have you been so long?"

"They told me as you were dead, dead of the fever, and buried," he gasped, his heart throbbing more quickly than ever, and his breath almost failing him as he spoke.

"Who said I was dead?" she asked, in mingled grief and anger.

"It was Cripple Jack," he answered, leaning against the door-post and bursting into tears, "here in this very place, and I've been mournin' after you, and we've been wanderin' up and down anywhere, without a place to shelter us, when you were here all the while!"

Come in, Don," she said, urgently, "come in at once. I'm not dead, and there's a home for you, and you shall tell me all about it when you've had something to eat."

"But there's little Dot," he replied, raising himself up, and turning away feebly to fetch her.

"Oh, she's lost," said Mrs. Clack, in a mournful voice; "Peggy lost her the very day before I came home from my holiday in the country, and she's never been heard of since."

"It was me as took her away," whispered Don; "she's been with me all along, and she's close by now. I'll go and fetch her."

But Dot had grown tired of being hid, and already she was running out to find Don, calling him loudly in her clear childish voice. He was trembling too greatly to go to meet her, but Mrs. Clack ran to bring her in, trembling almost as much as Don for very joy. What would Hagar feel when she found the child? But Mrs. Clack's joy faded away as she watched how slowly and painfully, and with what difficult steps, Don climbed the steep staircase to the room above.

He sank down breathless and exhausted on his old seat by the fire-side. Still it was with a happy smile that he looked round the room. It was exactly the same as in the old times; not a thing was altered. Mrs. Clack herself looked no older. Was it ten months since he had last seen them, or years instead of months? The tears dimmed his eyes a little as he gazed about him, and felt the comfort of the fire stealing through his numbed and weary frame. He could not speak, for his happiness was beyond words.

Mrs. Clack too was happy, though there was so terrible a change in Don. He was at home once more, and she could take care of him and nurse him well. Then there was Hagar's happiness to think of, ay, and Abbott's. Little Dot was standing close by Don, leaning half shyly against him, as she scrutinised Mrs. Clack's strange face, and though she was not so rosy as she had been in the summer, she was yet healthy-looking, and her little hands and arms were plump and firm. She made Don's face seem still more pinched and hunger-bitten. His eyes met Mrs. Clack's as she stood gazing fixedly upon them both.

"Cripple Jack told me as little Dot was to be taken to the workhouse," he said, with a faint light breaking in his dim eyes, and with a smile playing on his face, "and I couldn't abear that. I couldn't leave her to go there, and I took her away with me. I've never forsook her, never! And now she'll never have to go there, never—never."

His voice failed him, but the smile did not pass away from his lips. He stroked little Dot's curls, feeling that never had there been such rest and satisfaction for him, after all his troubles and his fears.

"Don't you talk no more till I've got tea ready," said Mrs. Clack, "and then you shall tell me all, and I'll tell you all. There's lots to tell."

She made haste to prepare tea, and ran down to send Peggy for some new bread, and a kippered herring, such as had been a rare feast for Don in former days. His eyes followed her restlessly wherever she moved about the room, as if he was afraid she would vanish out of his sight. And he was partly afraid. Was this a dream? or were the last ten months the dream? His brain felt too bewildered to, answer the question.

But when the tea was poured out, and steamed fragrantly before him, and the food was heaped up on his plate, he could not swallow a mouthful. The mere effort seemed to choke and suffocate him. He was too tired to be hungry, he said, and he stretched himself on the hearth, with his eyes still fastened upon Mrs. Clack and Dot as they sat at the table, listening to them and laughing feebly once or twice when Dot began chattering gaily, as if she was quite at home. When the meal was over, and Mrs. Clack drew her chair up to the fire, with Dot upon her lap, he lay quietly on the hearth in great contentment, gazing up into the two faces which were dearest to him in all the world.

"Ay, I've lots to tell you," he said, with a half sigh, "but I'm too tired now. And there's lots o' things I wanted to ask you, only I thought as you was dead. You're a clever woman, Mrs. Clack; and you can tell. There's God—did He really send His Son out of heaven, you know, to come here, and live like us?"

"Ay, he did," answered Mrs. Clack, "only we're always forgettin' it, and goin' on as if it wasn't true. God loved us, and sent His Son Jesus Christ, and Jesus Christ loved us, and came to save us."

"Oh, is that true?" he asked, eagerly, half raising himself from the floor; "did Jesus really come to save us, and to help us to be good? They told me so, but it was too good to be true. Is He the Son of Man that came to seek and to save them that are lost?"

"Yes," she answered, solemnly, "it's all true. It was a hard thing for Him to do; but He never gave up. He lived like us; and then He finished by dying on the cross for our sakes. He's done all He could for us, He was so sorry for us that He couldn't leave us or forsake us, because He loved us."

"No, He couldn't forsake us," said Don, with a shining face. "I know it's true now. I couldn't never have forsook little Dot."

He asked no more of the questions he had longed to have answered, for the exertion of speaking was too great for him. But Mrs. Clack told him of her holiday in the country, with all its pleasant surprises and memories of her own childhood, and Don enjoyed listening to them, remembering all the while the wonders of his own sojourn at the sea-side, which he would tell to her in return as soon as he was a little more rested. She went on to describe to him Hagar's heart-broken grief over her lost child, and the tears stood in his eyes again as he heard of it. He said how sorry he was that he had taken Dot away, yet he had done it to save her from a fate he dreaded, and Mrs. Clack laid her hand fondly on his head, and said, "God bless you, Don!"

"We'll start first thing in the morning," she said, "and take Dot home to her mother. It's Sunday morning, too, and may be Mr. Abbott's at home. Hagar was here last night, helping me to mend some gowns, and she told me as she is to be married to Mr. Abbott when Easter comes; but her heart's as heavy as can be for little Dot's sake, and she couldn't think she could ever be happy again, even with him. And, oh! Don, I'd like you to grow up to be a man like him! P'raps he'll get you a place on the railway, with settled work. I never thought there could be men like him; if he wasn't so strong and hearty, I should be afraid he'd not be long for this world, as folks say."

"That's what folks said of me," remarked Don, "and I felt as if I couldn't die before seeing the old place, so me and Dot came off here at once."

"Are you ill, Don?" she asked, anxiously.

"Oh no, only quite tired; I shall sleep well to-night, and it 'll be all right in the morning. Everything is right now, and we'll take Dot to Mrs. Haggar. But it'll be very hard to part with my little gel"

Dot had fallen asleep beside him on the hearth, and the fire-light shone full on her pretty face. Don gazed on her with a deep mute tenderness shining through his eyes, and Mrs. Clack felt as if some great and marvellous change had passed upon him.

"I've lots to learn," he said, after a long silence. "I know nothink at all save that God loves us, and sent His Son to us, and He is the Son of Man that came to seek and to save them that are lost. That's all I know. I must set to work and learn hard."

It was growing late before Don, in his weariness, roused himself up to the exertion of going downstairs to the coach-house beneath and his hard mattress, on which he had slept so soundly in old times. Dot woke up when he stirred, and would not be parted from him, crying and fretting till Mrs. Clack told Don to take her with him. She watched them down the steep staircase, waiting to put out the gas, and saw how fond and careful Don was of the little child, though he had to cling to the wall himself to get down. He turned to look at her before passing into the place below, and she saw his face bright and happy with a smile of utter content. It brought the tears to her eyes, and she could scarcely answer his last "Good-night."

It seemed to Don almost like heaven to get back once more to his old shelter. He had been tossed to and fro so long, sleeping, if he was under a roof at all, in some crowded lodging-house, that this quiet place, dimly lighted by a little candle, was like a long-wished-for haven of rest and tranquillity to him. The dark corners were scarcely touched by the feeble glimmer of his light, and the unpaved floor was damp under his feet, but it was here that he felt at home, and no other spot in all the wealthy dwelling-places of London could have given to him the same perfect sense of satisfaction and peace. He had not been it since old Lister had died there, on the self-same mattress on which little Dot was soon fast asleep; and Don sat down to rest himself, amid to think over all that night, and what old Lister had said before he crossed the threshold of the other world. Don knew now what he had only heard for the first time then. In this world he had Mrs. Clack and little Dot to love and be loved by; in the other world there were God and Jesus Christ who loved him, and whom he loved already. His whole soul was full of happiness and rest. Could there be anything better for him to learn? "O God!" he whispered, as he lay down weariedly beside little Dot, "I know nothink yet; only you love me, and I thank you."

Mrs. Clack was astir early in the morning, and took care to have a tempting breakfast ready for Don as soon as he awoke. She heard through the floor between her room and the coach-house, that Dot was awake, and calling to him to take her up, and she went quietly downstairs with a light in her hand to fetch the little child away, if she could persuade her to come without disturbing Don. He was very fast asleep, though Dot was sitting up beside him, crying in a half-frightened tone, as she patted his pinched face, and called "Old Don!" Mis. Clack stepped cautiously to the bed-side, and laid her hand very gently on the wasted forehead, which felt icy-cold to her fingers.

Don was dead.

Chapter XVIII

Grief and Gladness

It was some time before Mrs. Clack could believe that what she dreaded was true, and, like little Dot, she called aloud, "Don! Don!" His white face was very peaceful, and his wasted frame lay restfully on the mattress, as though he were still only sleeping, and would rouse up presently, if they only called him loud enough. In the flickering light of her candle she almost fancied his lips smiled faintly, as Dot's little hands stroked his face; but in her inmost heart she knew that he was gone from this world's grief and gloom, though it had been by a thorny path. Already he knew more than all earthly teachers could tell him. He was gone to be taught by God Himself.

Mrs. Clack went back upstairs, carrying the crying child, but she herself was too troubled for tears.

It was Sunday morning, and the mews was quieter on week-days, as most of its inhabitants were still slumbering. Nobody had seen Don come back the night before; and with the old habits of reserve yet clinging to her, she had not told any one, even when she had sent Peggy on her errand. She felt reluctant to rouse any of them to hear the sad news. There was no doubt in her mind that Don had been dying slowly of starvation, but oh! was she to blame in not sending for a doctor last night when he was too tired to swallow the food she offered to him? Could he have been saved if she had listened to the fears her heart had whispered? It was clear from what little Dot said that he had not touched a morsel of food all the day, and it was only too probable that many hours had passed since he had taken anything to nourish life. She knew the sad secret of how many hours it is safe to go without food. It was no new thing to her to discover that the poor may slowly famish from the want of things necessary to life, until they grow unconscious of the certain death that is stealthily lying in wait for them; when their resolution breaks down, and they accept the dreaded shelter of the workhouse, too late.

Mrs. Clack determined upon going at once to consult with Abbott, and to take Dot to her mother, before telling her trouble to any one else. It was not a very cold morning, but the clouds were low, and the sky gloomy as Mrs. Clack and Dot crossed the Kensington Gardens. The child with some recollection of the place, left her side to run among the trees, hiding herself behind them, and calling gleefully to the sad old woman, whose heart was filled with sorrow and awe. But she did not check her merriment; for had not Don given his life to save her? And her laughter and happiness would be very dear to Don; he would not wish her to be gloomy and weeping, even for his sake.

The church bells were beginning their first chimes for the morning service when she reached the house where Abbott was still living on the ground floor, and Hagar in her little room under the roof. She hesitated for a minute, and then led Dot down the area steps, and knocked at Abbott's door. It was opened immediately; for he was at home, and ready to go out as soon as he heard his cousin and Hagar leaving the house by their, entrance above. Mrs. Clack pushed Dot forward, and for the first time the tears welled up to her eyes, and sobs came to her lips.

"There's little Dot," she cried; "but oh! Don is dead, starved to death! He's been famishing himself to take care of her, and he's dead."

"Don dead?" he repeated; "starved to death? And little Dot here. Hush! there's Hagar coming downstairs. Hagar," he cried, hastening to the foot of the staircase, "don't set off just yet; wait till I come to you."

He placed Mrs. Clack in his mother's old arm-chair, and raised Dot into his arms, wondering how he was to break the glad news to Hagar, that the child was found, just as they were giving up all hope. But even in these first moments of joy it was plain to him that there was a grief behind it, which must cast a shadow over it for ever. He had never seen Don, but he had heard much about him, and he knew how dear he was to Mrs. Clack. And now she was weeping bitterly, and sobbing out that he was dead.

"He brought Dot home to me last night," she said; "and I found him this morning lyin' dead in his bed with a smile on his face, and I came away to you, and never told anybody, and there he is now, this minute, as if he was only sleepin.'"

"Where is he?" asked Abbott.

"On the mattress where he always used to sleep," she answered; "and I could almost fancy he was alive, and it 'ud be all right if I went home again and called him. But he's dead; died in his sleep, and me never hearin' a cry or a groan. Oh! what shall I do?"

"Old Don's fast asleep," said little Dot; "I called him, and he never spoke. I couldn't make him open his eyes. Poor old Don!"

"Mrs. Clack," said Abbott, "I must fetch Hagar down, and let her have her little child again. She never knew Don, and you must bear with her a little if she thinks of nothing, just at present, except Dot. You know as well as I do how she's been pining after her, and how she's almost given up all hope. I will go and bring her here."

He found Hagar standing at the open door, waiting for him, as he had asked her, and wondering what made him so late this Sunday morning. He led her downstairs, to the door of the kitchen where Mrs. Clack and Dot were, hardly knowing what to say to her.

"Hagar," he said, in a hurried yet hesitating manner; "Mrs. Clack is here; she has brought something for you,'

"Brought something for me!" repeated Hagar.

"Yes, a thing you have longed for, and despaired of, and given up all hopes of," he answered. "Something that you cannot be happy without. Cannot you guess, Hagar?"

She stood motionless, with her hand upon the fastening of the door. All the colour faded away from her face, though an eager and almost wild light shone in her eyes. It seemed to her barely possible to utter a word, and yet her lips faltered out, "Not my little Dot?"

Yes," he said.

It was not her hand but his that opened the door, for all the strength had forsaken her. But when her eyes fell upon Dot, her little girl, so long ago forsaken, as lost, and so sorrowfully sought after, she cried with a very sharp and piercing cry, and sank down on her knees before her, hardly able to clasp her in her trembling arms.

"Oh, my darling! my little child, my own little Dot! Now I know," she sobbed, "at last, that God has forgiven me."

"Go away!" said Dot, pushing her back, and struggling to free herself from her clasp; "go away. I want old Don. I want to go and wake up old Don."

It was a sudden and wholesome check upon the excess of Hagar's gladness. Her child had forgotten her, the child she had deserted. Dot looked on her merely as a stranger, and cried to go back to the boy who was known only by name to Hagar. She rose up from the ground where she had knelt and sank down on a chair gazing wistfully at Dot. There was a great silence in the place; no one spoke to her, and when she looked up astonished, she saw that Mrs. Clack was weeping bitterly, and Abbott's face was sad.

"What is the matter?" she asked, in a tumult of great joy, and sorrow and vague dread.

"It's only me and Don," answered Mrs. Clack; "I felt as he'd be almost like a son to me when he came back. It's him as has taken care of Dot, and he brought her home again last night in the dusk. I was sittin' by the fire, thinkin' of him, when I heard his knock, ay, I was sure it was his knock,' at the door, and I went down to let him in and give him a welcome. But it looked like a ghost at the door, tall and thin, and a white face, and great starin' eyes as bright as stars—I could hardly believe it was Don. And when he'd climbed the stairs, and could speak a little, he told me Cripple Jack had made him believe I was dead and buried, and Dot was goin' to be sent to the workhouse. So to save her he stole her away, and they've been livin' anyhow they could at the East End, nights and nights never in a bed, and days and days with hardly a morsel to eat; only he went short himself that Dot might have enough. And he never forsook her. And he overworked himself, and starved himself" she sobbed, her voice breaking down when she uttered the word "starved."

"I'll take care of him," cried Hagar; "I'll be good to him as long as he lives. Oh! if I'd only been true like him."

"He's dead," said Mrs. Clack, after a short silence; "I've known other folks die in that way. They drop off unawares to themselves. It's hard to bear hunger at first, but they get used to it after a while, and they never think it's killing them. I'm sure Don didn't think he was so near dyin', though he said folks told him he wasn't long for this world. He bid me good night quite joyful, and I waited and listened till he'd put his candle out, and him and Dot were quite quiet. If he'd only stirred or groaned in the night I couldn't help hearin' him. But he went away in his sleep, and now surely he is where the Lord Jesus is, though he knew so little about Him. He was longin' to learn more about Him, and now he sees His face, maybe."

It seemed to bring the other world very near to them, as, with a strange sense of awe and sorrow, they thought of Don standing in the presence of the Saviour, whose footsteps he had followed so faithfully, though he had not known it. "Greater love hath no man than this, that he lay down his life for his friends." And Don had possessed and manifested this love. Why should they wish him back again to the troubles and sorrows of this sinful world? He had fought his fight, and finished his course; he had kept what he knew of the faith. They could not have spoken a word to call him back again into the thick of the battle.

They set out for the low, dark coach-house, where his body lay. The nearest way was through Kensington Gardens, and every step brought back to Hagar the sick despair that had conquered her, when she had abandoned her father and little Dot. She had east away her burden and Don had taken it up. But she knew more now of the loving-kindness of God which never fails, even if it leads His children homewards along a path as full of gloom and grief as that which Don had trodden.

"But He can't undo the wicked things we've done," she said, half aloud; "it will never be the same as if I hadn't forsook them. If I'd kept true, Don would be alive now. It seems as if little Dot belonged more to him by rights than to me."

There was but a dim light in the coach-house, though it was full noon-day when they entered it, but it was light enough to see Don's calm pale face, and the peaceful smile lingering upon it. He had passed away in a tranquil sleep, and his weary body was lying for ever at rest. There was no more labour for the hands to do, no rough road for the feet to tread. There would never more be hunger and thirst for him, no houselessness nor friendlessness. He was gone home to his Father, God.

"He'll 'lever grow up to be a man now," whispered Mrs. Clack, mournfully; "but I know he'd have made a good man, and he'd have been like a son to me."

Chapter XIX

A Shameful Verdict

It was necessary to have an inquest held on the death of the homeless and nameless boy; and the usual verdict of death through starvation was returned.

This verdict is growing common enough to lose its power of giving a shock to the hundreds of thousands of hearths where comfort and ease abound. Last year seventy-seven persons died from this cause in London alone. But Mrs. Clack had some few visitors who came, with aching hearts, to learn all the particulars of Don's early death, and to see if anything could be done to prevent such deaths in the future. To perish of hunger in the midst of plenty such as the world never knew before. To die of famine and the want of all things, whilst our river is thronged with heavily-laden ships coming in day after day, bringing stores of corn and food from the furthest ends of the earth! To be stinted in the absolute necessaries of life, whilst luxury and waste run riot on every hand, whilst hundreds of tons of food are thrown away! That was terrible. Christ had come amongst us, in the form of one of the least of His brethren; he had been hungry, and we had not fed him; naked, and we clothed him not; a stranger, and we took him not in.

There are charities enough provided for rescuing the perishing; but in the chain there is a link lost somewhere, which causes all the machinery of charity to fail in reaching the deep necessities of the silent poor. It may be, as Mrs. Clack said, that Don starved and died unawares, Death creeping along this by-path so stealthily that the destined victim knows nothing of his approach. But those who heard of Don felt it to be an infamy to the greatest and richest city in the world, a Christian city, that one of its children should famish in its streets.

They buried him in the grave which Abbott had bought for his mother, and where Hagar's baby was lying; for they could not bear the thought of laying him in a common grave, where every trace of his last resting-place would presently be lost. He had no name that they could put upon the headstone; but they added a new inscription to that already upon it, one which would remind them of him whenever they came to the spot: "He shall hunger no more, neither thirst any more; and God shall wipe away all tears from his eyes."

After Hagar and Abbott had been married a few months, they persuaded Mrs. Clack to give up her old home in the mews and her toilsome business, and to come and live in the pleasant attic which had been Hagar's place of refuge. They had not forgotten that Don would have been like a son to her; and they felt as if they were in duty bound to make up to her, as far as possible, what she had lost in him. She had made some provision for her old age, which would make her partly independent of them; but they could look better after her comfort and welfare if she was under the same roof, they said.

As time passed on Hagar grew happier; for though she could never forget the past, her thoughts no longer brooded over it. She had learned to know God better, and to trust in Him; and even if He had required her to pass again through the sharp trial she had failed in before, she would have been willing to meet it. She was ready to endure the cross, despising the shame.

Little Dot was never weary of listening to the story of Don's great love for her; and Mrs. Clack was fond of telling it. The child's memory could not keep the recollection of those hard times; and she would have forgotten Don himself, if it had not been for the oft-repeated story. Hagar herself would sometimes lay aside her work, and draw near to hear it, in spite of the pain it stirred in her heart.

"Don loved you, and lost his life for you," Hagar would say to her child, with a sad smile upon her face.

But oh, if it had not been all a mistake! If he'd only come back a day later, when Mrs. Clack had got home. Or if he hadn't believed Cripple Jack, Don might have been alive now!"

"Ay," said Abbott, one day when she said this in his hearing, "and yet it brought Don nearer to being like our Lord Jesus Christ than if he'd lived comfortable amongst us, and grown up into a man. 'Greater love hath no man than this, that he lay down his life for his friends.' And Hagar," he continued, in a lower tone of mingled joy and reverence, "it was through no mistake, and no lie, like that which caused poor Don's death, but because He knew there was no other way to bring us back to God, that Jesus Christ came and 'laid down His life for us.'"

SARAH SMITH (writing as Hesba Stretton) – A CONCISE BIBLIOGRAPHY

Short Stories & Periodicals
The Lucky Leg (19th March 1859)
The Ghost in the Clock Room (Christmas, 1859)
The Postmaster's Daughter (All the Year Round, 5th November 1859)
A Provincial Post Office (All the Year Round, 28 February 1863)
Jessica's First Prayer (Sunday at Home, July 1866)
The Travelling Post-Office (All the Year Round, Mugby Junction, December 1866)
Jessica's Mother (1867)

Books

Fern's Hollow (1864)
Enoch Roden's Training (1865)
The Children of Cloverley (1865)
Jessica's First Prayer (Sunday at Home, July 1866)
The Fishers of Derby Haven (1866)
Jessica's Mother (Periodical 1867, book 1904)
Pilgrim Street (1867)
Little Meg's Children (1868)
Alone in London (1869)
Nellie's Dark Days (1870)
The Doctor's Dilemma (1872)
The King's Servants (1873)
Lost Gip (1873
Cassy (1874)
Brought Home (1875)
In Prison and Out (1878)
Two Secrets (1882)
The Lord's Purse-Bearers (1883)
Sam Franklin's Savings Bank (1888)
Little Meg's Children (1905)
The Christmas Child (1909 in US)

Other Works

Brought Home
Cobwebs And Cables

www.ingramcontent.com/pod-product-compliance
Lightning Source LLC
Chambersburg PA
CBHW061457170626
46811CB00004B/1549